The Haunted Cove

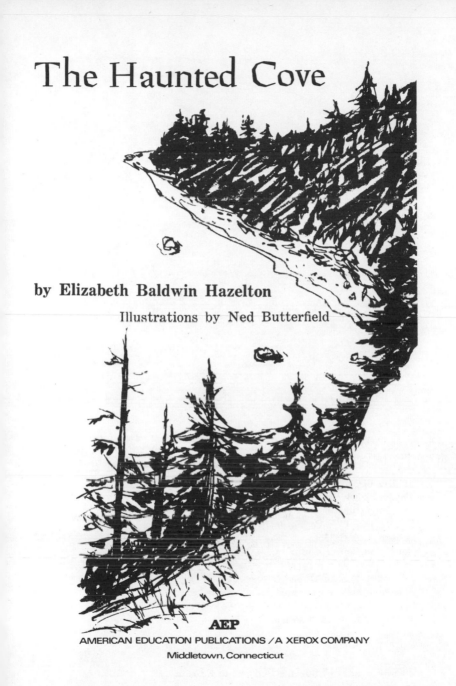

by Elizabeth Baldwin Hazelton

Illustrations by Ned Butterfield

AEP
AMERICAN EDUCATION PUBLICATIONS / A XEROX COMPANY
Middletown, Connecticut

To J. A. L.

who has a special magic

Publishing, Executive, and Editorial Offices:
American Education Publications,
245 Long Hill Road
Middletown, Connecticut 06457
Subscription Offices:
Education Center, Columbus, Ohio 43216

Library of Congress Catalog Card Number: 70-179042

Weekly Reader Children's Book Club Edition
Intermediate Division

CONTENTS

1

THE MAGIC NUMBER

Mrs. MacAlistaire turned the car onto the narrow gravel road that looped down from the highway to the cliffs above the sea. Kevin and Christie could hardly wait for her to reach the cottage that was to be theirs for a month-long holiday on the Oregon coast. Already they could glimpse the cool blue of the ocean between the dark green shapes of wind-bent trees.

The road curved, and they saw seven little cottages scattered along the rim of the cliff.

"Which is ours, Mom?" asked Kevin.

Mrs. MacAlistaire looked at her son's dark eyes, bright and eager beneath a thatch of brown, springy hair.

"Guess!" she said, her own eyes twinkling.

Kevin and Christie studied the houses carefully as the car approached them. None of them were new; they had a gray, weathered look. But somehow it made them all the more appealing, as if they'd stood firmly against the wintry blasts of many storms and could be depended upon to stand through many more.

"The third one," said Kevin. It was the most dilapidated, but he liked it because it rose boldly upon a point of rock, without a single tree to shelter it, as

though it had deliberately chosen to face the biting edge of wind-blown sands and cold salt spray.

"I hope it's the fifth!" Christie said. Her blue eyes sparkled and her honey-blonde hair swirled around her shoulders as she twisted in her seat to get a better view. She liked the fifth house because it was nestled into a little hollow below the top of the cliff, and almost hidden by a leaning circle of pines.

"Hm–m," said Mrs. MacAlistaire thoughtfully, "if those are your choices, you may both prefer to go back inland to the city, where the temperature today was 103!"

"Oh, boy, not me!" declared Kevin. "I'll take any one of them. I'd even settle for a shed."

Already his mother had driven past the third house, and the fourth, and now she was passing the

6

fifth. She kept driving north. There were only two left.

Christie held her breath as they passed the sixth cottage. "It's the seventh!" she shouted suddenly. "Oh, Mommy, I'm glad you chose that one. It's the perfect number!"

"Seven?" asked Kevin in surprise. "What's special about that?"

"You might say it's a sort of magic number," his mother explained. "The ancients thought it sacred, and even today many people believe it to be lucky."

"Living in the seventh house is going to bring us a wonderful holiday," Christie bubbled excitedly. Just thinking about it sent a shiver of anticipation down her spine.

Kevin didn't bother to comment. He was used to his sister's romantic notions and generally unimpressed by them. His mother had braked the car to a stop in front of the garage, and he opened the door and bounded out.

The seventh cottage was solidly anchored to the top of the cliff, and beneath the shade of its hemlocks and red cedars a little garden had grown wild. Separating it from the road, an old split-rail fence sagged against a crooked gate. But inside, the untended garden had been nurtured by coastal mists and rains, and azaleas and rhododendron bushes were still blooming in bright clusters of pink and rose.

A stone-lined path wound through uncut grasses quilted with white and purple and yellow wildflowers. At the front door a rusty ship's bell waited

7

to be rung. Kevin ran up the path and gave the clapper a yank. While the metal sang out, he followed the path around to the side of the house and discovered that it had two stories.

The main part of the cottage was built on the level of the road, but a lower floor had been set into the sloping cliff beneath it. From where he stood, a wooden stairway led past it down the cliff. But it was the view beyond that made him gasp.

"Wow!" he exclaimed.

Christie, who had stopped to admire the flowers, ran to stand beside him at the edge of the cliff, and their mother followed. Below them, the ocean was rolling in long foaming breakers onto a wide sandy beach. Out in the midst of the cresting waves, huge gray rocks rose up out of the water like haystacks.

"Golly!" Christie breathed softly. "It's even more beautiful than I imagined. And look—there!"

Kevin and his mother raised their eyes to follow Christie's glance and saw the sun. It hung like a great orange ball caught in the twisted branches of a single shore pine.

Kevin was aching to get down to the shore. "Mom," he asked, "couldn't we wait about unloading the car and go down on the beach for a while?"

"Just until after sunset," pleaded Christie, who was as eager as he.

"I don't know why not; we have plenty of time," Mrs. MacAlistaire conceded cheerfully.

Kevin was halfway down the cottage stairs before she had finished the sentence.

"I'll go in and open the windows," his mother went on. "It's probably warm and stuffy inside."

"Aren't you coming down?" asked Christie.

"Not this evening," said her mother. "Five hours is a lot of driving through the heat." She was looking at the sundeck on the roof of the lower story. "I think I'll stretch out on that old couch on the deck and let the breezes blow over me." She put her arm lovingly around Christie's shoulders. "You run along and see if you can discover the beginning of the magic."

Christie leaned against her mother for a moment, breathing in the fresh sea air. "I can smell it already," she said. "It's the scent of cedars and salt and— something else. Mysterious sea creatures, maybe?"

"Maybe." Her mother smiled and touched Christie's forehead lightly with her lips.

Christie smiled back, then bolted down the steps.

At the foot of the stairs great logs, bleached white by sun and sea, lay piled one upon another like fallen giants. As Christie climbed over them, she thought of what terrible winds and raging waves it must have taken to push such a floating forest across the wide beach to the base of the cliff, and then stack them up like so many toothpicks. In a storm like that a person would be drowned or blown away. She wondered if there could ever be such a storm in the summer.

When she had clambered over the last log, she saw Kevin perched on an uprooted stump, taking off his tennis shoes.

"The tide's out," he said. "I'm going wading."

Christie took off her shoes and socks and followed him to the water's edge. The sea swirled in, covering their feet with a thin layer of cold, foaming bubbles.

9

The sun was slanting down toward the horizon, making rainbows in the foam. While Christie watched the delicate colors bubbling around her toes, a young couple ran through the water in front of them.

The man was tall, with thick red hair and a red beard, and he wore Levi's cut off at the knees. The girl was pretty, with straight brown hair that hung down to her waist, and she was wearing a long, full dress that fell free from her shoulders. As she ran, she tried to hold it above the gentle surf.

Kevin and Christie watched them as they kept running toward the base of the great headland that thrust itself out into the sea, closing this cove off from the next one, to the north.

When the breakers rolled in, they smashed high against the rock face of the land, but as the sea drew back, there was a moment when the water was only knee high. In that moment, the young man ran through, and with a shriek, the girl ran after him. A big comber rushed in behind her, and for an instant she was hidden by the great splattering of foam.

As the waters sucked back, Kevin and Christie saw the man and girl once more, still running through the water with the girl's dress billowing out behind her. Then they disappeared around the headland.

"Let's follow them," said Kevin, starting toward the promontory. "I want to see what's in the next cove."

"No—wait, Kevin!" Christie protested. "The waves are too big and the tide's turning."

But Kevin had already run beyond where he could hear her. He was two years older than she, with longer legs, and she had to run desperately hard to try to catch him.

He had reached the outer edge of the passage and stopped, watching for the moment when the water would slide back, when Christie screamed, "Kevin—wait!"

He looked back at her for an instant. Then he decided to ignore her warning. When he turned again to the headland, a giant wave was hurling itself thirty feet up the rock face of the cliff. He ducked back, but not in time to escape the drenching fall of water.

Christie reached him, too out of breath to speak. Finally she said, "If you'd gone through that time, you'd be dead."

"It just happened to be a big one," he said, a bit shaken.

"That was the seventh wave," said a voice behind them.

They turned and saw a girl in a blouse and skirt splashed with bright patches of red and yellow and purple and orange. Her dark hair fell loosely over her shoulders, and with the olive tan of her skin, she looked almost like a gypsy. Except for her pale gray eyes. She was as tall as Kevin, and Christie thought she looked older. He was twelve. She must be at least thirteen, maybe more.

"The seventh wave is always the biggest," she said, "but in this place there'll be seven more like the seventh. Watch and see!"

They followed her eyes to where the breakers were rolling in toward the headland.

"That's the second," she said.

It smashed against the rock and sent up a white tower of foam as high as the one before it.

The three of them stood watching and counting. One by one, the powerful waves rolled in to hurl the great weight of their waters against the rock. Three —four—five—six—seven!

"You see?" the girl said.

It was true. There had been seven waves added to the seventh, all of them so towering that no one could have passed around the headland without being smashed against the cliff. A human body would have been crushed and broken beyond saving.

"You said 'the seventh wave is always the biggest, but in this place there'll be seven more like the seventh,'" Kevin reminded the girl.

"And you just saw it happen," she said.

"I know," Kevin admitted. "But what did you mean: '*in this place*'? Why is this place any different from any other?"

"Because it's haunted!" the girl declared.

"Haunted!" Kevin scoffed.

"Haunted!" Christie whispered at the same instant. Her heart felt as if it had turned a somersault inside her chest.

"Do you expect me to believe that?" demanded Kevin.

"You can ask anyone who lives in this town," the girl insisted. "The cove beyond this headland has been haunted for nearly a hundred years. And that

12

couple who ran into it before the seventh wave will never come back."

"You're crazy!" said Kevin.

"Oh, no I'm not!" the girl bristled. "That's why seven waves followed the seventh. So they couldn't return before it was too late."

"Too late for what?" demanded Kevin.

"Look at the water now," said the girl, ignoring him.

They looked and saw that even when it slid back briefly between breakers, it was very deep and rough—far over a man's head. And the sea churned and frothed as if there were dangerous riptides beneath the surface.

"All right—so they can't get back now," Kevin admitted, "but when the tide goes out again, they can run back the same way they ran in."

"If you think so, sit here all night and wait for them. And all day tomorrow and the next night, if you want to," the girl told him. "But you'll see—they won't come back."

"Then they'll get out some other way," reasoned Kevin.

"There *is* no other way," said the girl. "At the north end of the cove, there's a bigger headland than this that juts much farther out into the sea. The water is even deeper and wilder than here. For almost one hundred years, every swimmer who's tried to get around it has drowned."

"Then they can climb up the cliff," Kevin suggested.

"It's too steep," the girl told him.

13

"If they can't get out, what will happen to them?" asked Christie.

"They'll just disappear," said the girl calmly.

"*Disappear!*" Kevin stared at her in utter astonishment and disbelief.

"Won't somebody look for them?" asked Christie.

The girl turned to scan the length of the beach behind them. Far down the cove in front of the first cottage, a man and woman were lying on blankets, reading, while three small children waded at the water's edge. There was no one else in sight.

"I don't think anyone saw them but us," said the girl.

"But we *did* see them," said Christie.

"We don't know who they are," said the girl. "They're not from around here. They must have come down from the highway. They'd have to be strangers, or they'd never have gone into that cove."

Christie thought of the young couple running through the water, looking so handsome—and so happy.

"It doesn't matter whether we know them or not," she insisted earnestly. "We saw them go in, and if they can't get out, then we'll have to help them."

"Sure," Kevin agreed. "We can call the police."

"It wouldn't do any good."

"Why not?" Kevin and Christie demanded, together.

"Because of the witch," the girl said.

"The witch!" Kevin laughed mockingly. "Now I know you're full of baloney!"

Christie didn't say anything, but her heart did another flip-flop. If this was the "magic" of cottage number seven, it was too much and happening too

14

soon. She hadn't even had time to get her bearings.

"That's why it wouldn't do any good to call the police," the girl was saying. "Because they'd be too late. By now, the witch has had plenty of time to work her evil magic."

"You're lying!" Kevin told her. "There aren't any witches any more. There haven't been for hundreds of years."

"That shows how ignorant you are," the girl said scornfully. "There are hundreds of witches all over the country—*covens* of them."

"What are covens?" Christie asked weakly.

"Gatherings," said the girl. "Like clubs. They meet and make potions and cast spells. Some are good witches and some are evil."

"What's the difference?" asked Christie.

"The good witches are kind people who make good spells," the girl explained, "and the evil witches are bad people who make spells that are harmful."

"And I suppose this one is an evil witch," said Kevin, still scoffing.

"Of course, and so was her great grandmother. It was she who put the first curse on the cove, about one hundred years ago, and sank a ship and drowned eleven men."

Christie felt her heart thump in her throat. "This witch," she said hesitantly. "Has anyone ever seen her?"

"Hardly anyone," said the girl, "but *I* have. And if you'll swear never to tell, I'll take you to where you can see her. This is the time of day when she comes out and stands on her rock in the middle of the sea—"

"The middle of the sea!" Kevin hooted.

"Yes," said the girl. "She stands out there at sunset and casts spells with her weird music. I have a secret place where I go to watch."

"Okay, let's go," Kevin declared decisively.

"Kevin—are you sure we should?" asked Christie doubtfully.

"Of course. Don't be a sissy!"

"All right," said the girl. "But first you'll have to take an oath. Put your right hand on your heart and swear you'll never tell anyone what you saw or heard, on penalty of being burned at the stake."

"You've got to be kidding," said Kevin.

"That's what they used to do to witches, and this is an oath about a witch. Either you take it, or we don't go," the girl declared firmly.

"Oh, all right," said Kevin disgustedly, "but it's silly."

"Put your hands on your hearts and say it," insisted the girl.

Kevin and Christie put their hands on their hearts.

"I swear I'll never tell anyone what I saw or heard, on penalty of being burned at the stake," Kevin said impatiently.

"I do, too," said Christie faintly.

"Say the *oath*!" the girl demanded.

Christie managed to say the words weakly, though her throat ached with the throbbing of her pulse.

"Okay, I'll take you," said the girl. "And you'll find out I'm not lying." She looked at Kevin and Christie intently, and her gray eyes seemed even paler than before. "You'll have to do exactly what I tell you and not make a sound," she warned, "because if the witch sees or hears us, we'll never get home again."

17

2
THE WITCH
AND HER SPELL

The girl led Kevin and Christie up a steep, winding trail that climbed the cliff from the beach to the road. At the top they stopped, gasping for breath. They were halfway between the seventh cottage and the headland, with another fifty yards to walk along the road. While they rested for a moment, they saw that the orange sun was turning red as it slipped down toward the sea.

"We'll have to hurry," the girl said, starting up the road.

"You haven't told us your name," said Christie, as they followed her.

"It's Mora," the girl said.

"Mora? I've never heard that name before," said Christie.

"I like it," the girl said.

"So do I," said Christie. "It's very pretty." And strange, too, Christie thought, like her eyes. The name and the eyes seemed to go together.

"My name's Christie," she remembered to tell Mora, "and you already know my brother's is Kevin."

Mora didn't answer. She began to run, and they trotted along beside her. When they reached the point where the headland extended out like an arm from the road to the sea, she slowed to a stop, and they stopped with her.

"We're almost to the haunted cove," she whispered, "but we can't go in if there's anyone around who could see us." She looked cautiously down the road behind them, and then ahead.

"There's nobody in sight," said Kevin.

"Okay, then we'll walk along as if we were going on past the cove," said Mora, "and when we reach a certain place, I'll duck into the woods and you follow me. But make it fast, before anybody can see us."

They started on with Mora in the lead. As they came closer to the cove, Kevin and Christie saw that the headland sloped up sharply from the road and its crest was hidden by a thick forest of hemlock and fir and pine.

Ahead of them, Mora darted suddenly into an opening between the trees and disappeared. Kevin and Christie tried to locate the same spot and sprint in after her, but when they had pushed their way through a long tangle of branches, Mora was nowhere to be seen. They stood alone in the shadowy gloom beneath the tall dark trees. The sad, sighing sound of the conifers filled the air around them, and the roar of the breakers was muffled and far away.

"I don't think we should have come," Christie whispered. "I have a spooky feeling about these woods, as if we'd walked into a secret place where no one is supposed to be."

"That's just because she told you it's haunted," said Kevin, but his voice was as hushed as hers.

"Don't you think it is?" asked Christie.

"Of course not," said Kevin, managing to get his voice back to normal. "Come on, we've got to find her."

He led the way through the dim forest. Christie followed, peering nervously between the long dark columns of trees. She was searching for Mora, but fearful that she might see something else. Neither she nor Kevin dared to risk calling out Mora's name.

At length they came head-on into a chain-link fence at least six feet high. Four rows of barbed wire were strung above it.

"If we have to go over that to see the witch, we may as well quit right now," said Kevin, eyeing it.

"We don't go over, we go *under*," said Mora, appearing out of nowhere.

"For Pete's sake, where have you been?" demanded Kevin impatiently.

"For Pete's sake, looking for you!" she snapped back. "You must have come in the wrong way."

"We tried to follow you," Christie began, "but—"

"Never mind. Follow me now or we'll miss the whole show," Mora said, moving swiftly along the fence.

"Does this fence go all around the property?" asked Kevin.

"You bet it does, and clear out to the tip of the other headland," said Mora.

"Then how in heck can we get under it?" asked Kevin.

"Because of that big rainstorm, two weeks ago," said Mora. "The earth got so wet there was a small rock slide, and it left a gap just big enough for one person to crawl through."

20

Kevin and Christie were hurrying along behind Mora, thrusting themselves between fence and undergrowth.

"Was that the first time you saw the witch—just two weeks ago?" asked Christie.

"Until then, there was no way *anybody* could see her, and I'm the only one who knows the secret now," declared Mora, "but I've come out every night since then, and I've seen plenty!"

Gradually the woods were thinning out on their side of the fence, and far below they could glimpse their own beach with its row of seven cottages. But on the witch's side, the forest was still thick. The branches of the trees overlapped, one upon the other, and they could see nothing at all of her cove.

They were coming perilously near to the end of the headland when Mora stopped abruptly. "This is it!" she said.

Beyond her feet they saw the place where a little stream had rushed down the slope and cut a gash in the earth beneath the fence. The loosened rock must have rolled with it over the cliff. The opening it left was barely big enough for a small person to crawl through.

Mora was already on her hands and knees. "I'll go first," she said, "and then I can help you. It's dangerous if you're not careful, because if you slip you'll go down over the cliff just like the rock slide."

Lying on her side, she grasped the fence and put her head in the opening under it. Then pulling and pushing, she wriggled through without mishap.

"You're next, Christie," she announced.

Mora's warning had made Christie apprehensive,

but she lay down as the older girl had done. "Don't let me slip, Kevin!" she pleaded.

"Don't worry, I won't," he promised.

Taking hold of the chain links, Christie put her head under the fence and began to push with her feet. It was then that the thing to be feared happened so swiftly that no one was prepared. The stones on which Christie was pushing gave way, and she slid down after them until she was hanging at arms length in the slippery gulley. Only her hands clinging desperately to the fence kept her from sliding down over the cliff.

"Help me!" she cried in terror.

Kevin seized the fence with his right hand to support himself, while with his left he reached down and caught hold of the belt of her dress. From the safe side of the fence, Mora tried to reach her wrists, but she could grasp only one.

"I don't know how strong your belt is," said Kevin. "It might break if I try to pull you up."

"You've got to pull me!" cried Christie frantically. "I can't hold on much longer. My arms are hurting terribly."

"You've *got* to hold on!" Kevin commanded.

On her side of the fence, Mora stretched out full length and reached under to take hold of Christie's right arm with both of hers.

"Go ahead, Kevin—pull!" she ordered. "If the belt breaks, I've got her arm and I won't let go."

Pulling cautiously at first, and then with all the strength he could summon to his left arm, Kevin pulled his sister back up the slope. The belt was holding. Christie was on her side again, her arms bent so that she could do some of the pulling herself.

"Now push with your feet," Kevin commanded.

Christie pushed, and this time the earth under her feet was firm. With Kevin's strength to help her, and with Mora pulling from the other side, they got her through the gap.

Inside the fence, Christie lay flat on the safe earth, sobbing from shock and relief.

After he had rested his strained arms for a moment, Kevin pulled himself through and collapsed beside her. Mora was pale beneath the olive tan of her skin, betraying the fear that she, too, had felt. They exchanged a silent look that meant: That was close!

But to his sister, Kevin said reassuringly, "You're all right now, Chris. It's over. You're safe."

Christie sat up, her blue eyes still wet with tears. "If it hadn't been for you two—" She looked with horror at the treacherous little gulley. If she had slipped down it and over the cliff, she'd have fallen more than two hundred feet to the rocks below.

"I'd never have let you go over," said Kevin. "I'd have held you by the hair of your head if I'd had to." Playfully, he grabbed a handful of her thick blonde hair and twisted it tightly around his fist.

"Maybe you'd better do that when we go back," said Christie, already thinking with dread of the dangerous return.

"I'll get you back safely," Kevin promised. "This time I'll be prepared."

"I've just thought of something," Mora said. "In a haunted place like this, there could be angry spirits."

Kevin wanted to tell Mora she was a kook, but then he remembered that she'd helped to save Christie. Instead, he said, "Where do you get all this stuff?"

"My sister has a book about witchcraft and I've studied it," said Mora seriously. "It tells everything about witches and demons and magic. That's how I know about evil spirits."

"What about them?" said Kevin.

"If they're angry, they can do you harm."

"Then maybe that's why I slipped," said Christie, in awe.

"You slipped because the stones went out from under you," Kevin said in disgust.

"How do we know there weren't spirits who caused the stones to move?" asked Mora.

"How do we know there's a witch, if we don't see her?" countered Kevin.

"You'll see her," Mora promised. "I can hear her music already. Listen!"

Kevin and Christie listened so intently they almost forgot to breathe. At first they could hear only the distant sound of the sea, and then over it came the high, silvery notes of a flute. A breaker roared in, drowning out the music, but they had heard it. There had been only three notes—odd and eerie, more like music dreamed than real—but now they could hardly wait to see the mysterious musician.

Mora led them up the slope. "When we get to the top," she warned, "stay in the shelter of the trees so the witch won't see you."

As she neared the crest of the slope, Mora dropped to her knees, and they both followed suit. Crawling up the last few feet, they peered over the top. Below them lay the witch's cove, looking every bit as haunted as they had imagined.

They couldn't see all of it, for the trees hung low and spread their branches wide, as if to hide the witch's secrets. But they saw the deep U-shape of the cove, with the headland on the other end reaching far out to sea. The sun-bleached driftwood on the shore was piled even higher than on their own beach, and the shapes of the logs and stumps were oddly twisted.

But it was the rocks out beyond the breakers that gave the cove its haunted look. They were unlike any rocks Kevin and Christie had ever seen. They rose high above the water in fantastic shapes, like enchanted creatures frozen there by an evil spell.

Some might have been huge prehistoric animals turned to stone as they tried to reach the shore. One was like an immense hand with five tapered fingers reaching up desperately, as though some drowning giant were sinking under the water for the last time.

Some looked like people bent down in grief and surrender. Cast into shadow by the red glow of the sunset sky behind them, the weird black shapes could be anything one chose to imagine—and all of them frightening.

But still they had not seen the witch, though now they heard again the same three notes, high and thin and eerie.

"You can't see her from here," said Mora. She stood up and moved cautiously toward a gnarled pine that clung to the rim of the cliff, its lower branches touching the ground.

"Don't go any closer to the edge," she warned. "The

26

precipice on this side is even steeper than on ours."

Carefully, she parted the branches at shoulder height. "There's the house," she said.

It was more gray and weatherbeaten than the cottages, and very old, and it looked exactly as Christie had imagined a haunted house should look. It was three stories high, with bay windows and gables and little round turrets with pointed roofs, and there were several tall chimneys built of stone. Across the front of the first story there was a long, wide porch that overlooked the cove and the sea.

"Aren't there any stairs from the house down to the beach?" asked Kevin.

"They're hidden," said Mora, her voice hushed,

"and nobody but the witch herself would dare go down them."

"Why not?" asked Kevin.

"Because they go down through a dark cavern in the rock—and do you know what's *in* that cavern?"

"What?" asked Christie breathlessly, half dreading to hear the answer.

"An urn with the bones of a dead man in it," whispered Mora, in awe, "and sometimes the ghosts of all the seamen who were drowned by that curse nearly one hundred years ago. Sometimes they meet there and make a terrible wailing cry that can be heard from this headland all the way to that one on the other end of the cove."

Christie gasped, but Kevin acted unimpressed.

"Did you get *that* out of your sister's book, too?" he asked tauntingly.

"No. I got that out of old newspapers right here in the town library," Mora snapped, her eyes sparking fire. "If you don't believe me, you can go there and read it yourself."

"Right now I'd rather see the witch," he said, with a grin that was intended to placate her.

"Then lie down on your stomach and lift up the bottom branch of the tree," she said, "but whatever you do, don't lean out."

Kevin lay down at the base of the tree, and Christie and Mora flattened themselves out beside him.

When he had lifted the branch, Kevin said, "I don't see anything but an empty beach."

"She's not on the beach," said Mora. "Look out to sea!"

They looked and saw a massive black rock rising like a square tower out of the water. On top of it grew one tree so twisted in shape that it looked as haunted as the rocks. Standing beneath it was a woman in a black cape, playing a flute.

Kevin and Christie stared in amazement. She was there, just as Mora had said, out on a rock beyond the rolling breakers, facing the sunset while she played her weird music.

But there was more than Mora had told them. Two white seagulls stood, one on each side of her, like sentinels, and at the base of her tower a herd of sea lions churned round and round as if the melody floating out of her flute made them want to dance.

"Are the gulls enchanted?" asked Christie.

"I think so," said Mora. "They're always with her on the rock or on her house. They never leave her. And the sea lions come whenever she plays a certain high note that's like a whistle."

In the red glow of the setting sun it was hard to be sure, but Christie thought she saw something glittering on the shoulders of the woman's cape.

"Are those gold disks on her shoulders?" she asked.

"I brought up my binoculars so I could see what they were," Mora told her, "and they're the sun and the moon. I think they're made out of pure gold. When she uses them, they must work powerful spells."

Kevin was astonished by all he saw, but one practical question bothered him most *how* did the black-cloaked woman get onto her rock? He could see no boat, nor were any stairs visible up the sheer walls

of her tower. But he didn't intend to ask Mora. He could guess what her answer would be: the witch, she would say *flew* out from her porch to the rock, or maybe even rode a cornstalk or a broom. He was not about to accept an answer like that, yet he couldn't come up with a better one.

"The young couple!" said Christie abruptly. "We forgot to look for them."

"If they'd been there, you'd have seen them," said Mora.

Christie jumped up and peered around the outer edge of the pine tree on its ocean side. From there, she could get a full view of the beach, and the sea rolling up onto it. The sun was hanging low over the water, making a narrow red path all the way to the shore.

Suddenly Kevin and Mora heard Christie let out a gasp and saw that her eyes were riveted on something far below.

"I see them!" she said. "He's running ahead just the way he was, and she's following behind him with her dress billowing out in back."

Kevin and Mora leaped up and ran to her side.

"Where?" asked Kevin.

"I can see his red hair and beard," she said, staring down at the sea. "He's out to his hips in the water and she's closer inshore."

"What are you talking about?" demanded Kevin. "I can't see them."

"They're right down there," Christie said, pointing to the sea at the foot of the cliff, "but the witch has turned them to stone!"

31

3
THE WHITE POTION

Kevin peered down at the two pillars of rock in disbelief. Their shapes *were* like the man and girl; he could even see the glow of red around the head of the one that stood hip deep in the water. But that color had to come from the glistening red sun path behind it. When the sun sank below the horizon, the red glow would be gone. The rocks would look like any others. It was Christie's imagination that had made him see the shapes of the man and girl, he told himself.

But Mora was convinced, not only because she, too, saw the resemblance between the young couple and the stone pillars, but for another reason.

"Those two rocks were never there before," she declared.

"You don't know that," Kevin challenged. "You could just have not seen them before. We didn't see them now till Christie came clear out from behind the tree."

"I've been out here for every sunset since I found the passage under the fence," Mora told him, "and

I've seen every rock in the cove. I know them all by heart. Those two were not here—not last night, not any time. They're the couple we saw, and she turned them to stone tonight."

They looked toward the witch on the tower, and at that moment she seemed to turn toward the three of them. From her flute came the highest, most piercing notes they had ever heard—seven in a row, all exactly alike. While they stood rooted to the spot, she blew again, the same shrill notes.

"Drop flat to the ground!" Mora commanded hoarsely. "And roll behind the tree."

Automatically, Kevin obeyed, but Christie waited a moment longer, fascinated and terrified by something she had seen.

"Chris!" hissed Kevin. "Drop flat!"

Chris fell flat on the ground and rolled toward them.

"She started to work her spell on us," said Mora, her face pale with fear. "Crawl down the slope as fast as you can. Maybe the earth will stop it."

When they had scrambled down the slope to the fence, Kevin said, "Let's get out of here. I'll go first, Chris, and brace myself so I can catch you."

"And I'll steady you from this side," said Mora.

But Christie didn't seem to hear them. There was a puzzled look in her eyes, and she was pressing the upper part of her right arm with the fingers of her left hand.

"What's the matter?" Kevin asked sharply.

"My arm," said Christie. "It's numb from my shoulder to my elbow."

"You must have hurt it when you dropped to the ground, up there," said Kevin, examining her arm for some sign of a bruise.

"I didn't hurt it," she said. "Just suddenly it was numb."

"But *after* you fell," he insisted, though he found no mark.

"It wasn't the fall," said Mora, a tremor in her voice. "It was the spell of the witch. You didn't drop down when I told you to, Christie. You just stood there, looking at her."

Christie wanted to tell them why she had stood there, and what she had seen, but she couldn't. Not yet.

"That's why your arm is numb," said Mora. "Her spell was already starting to turn it to stone. If you hadn't gotten down behind the slope just in time—"

"That's looney!" said Kevin.

"No it isn't!" Mora insisted. "She works her magic with those shrill notes from her flute. They're like invisible arrows, and one of them must have struck your arm."

"It didn't leave any mark," Kevin reminded her.

"Of course not," said Mora impatiently. "Witch arrows never leave marks. They just leave a numb place that has no feeling. If you hadn't dropped down when you did, you'd be a stone pillar standing up there, right now—just like that couple on the shore."

"You mean it will stay numb forever?" asked Christie fearfully.

"For gosh sake, Chris," said Kevin irritably, "don't tell me you believe all that dumb stuff. You hurt your arm when you fell, that's all—or when you had that bad time going under the fence. It'll be all right in a day or two."

"I can make it all right, at sunrise," said Mora mysteriously. "I can make a *magic* potion and say a spell that will heal it."

"You can?" asked Christie hopefully.

"Yes," said Mora. "That's why I'm studying witch-craft. So I can be a good witch, and help people."

"If you want to be so helpful," said Kevin, "you can use some of your 'magic' now to help me get Chris under this fence."

Very cautiously, he slipped under and then braced himself to catch his sister as she followed him. Moments later all three had made it safely and were on their way back through the woods.

The sun had gone down, and the shadows beneath the trees were already deeper than they had been before. The silence seemed deeper, too, and somehow more menacing. They walked softly but quickly, and no one spoke until just before they reached the road.

Then Mora took hold of Christie's arm and drew her back behind a tree. "Is it still numb?" she asked in a whisper.

Christie nodded.

"I know Kevin doesn't believe me," Mora said quickly, "but it's true—I *do* know about magic. It's all in my sister's notebook. I've memorized every spell, and I know how to make the healing potions and do the rituals. If you'll meet me at sunrise—"

"At sunrise?" Christie asked in surprise.

"For *good* magic," Mora explained, "the potions

have to be made just before sunrise, and the spell works best if it's done just as the sun is coming up."

Kevin had reached the road, and discovered that the girls weren't behind him. "Chris!" he called. "Come on. Mom'll be worried."

"Will you meet me?" Mora whispered.

"I don't know whether I can," said Christie doubtfully.

"If you don't, your arm may get worse," Mora warned, "but I can break the evil spell if you'll meet me here at sunrise."

"Here!" Christie looked around her at the dark woods and shivered.

"It's supposed to be done in a sacred grove," said Mora.

"But this isn't—" Christie protested.

"Yes it is," Mora whispered. "I've found a secret place and said the spells that make it sacred for my magic. I'll meet you here and take you to it."

"Chris! Where are you?" Kevin was coming back in search of them.

"I've got to go," Christie whispered.

"Will you come at sunrise?"

"If I can, but—"

"Listen," Mora whispered hastily, "in your cottage, the big bedroom is upstairs, so you and Kevin will sleep in the bunk bedrooms downstairs. They both have doors onto the porch. After dark, leave your door open a crack, and I'll bring you a charm to protect you through the night, and tell you the exact time of sunrise—"

"Chris! Mora!" Kevin was calling from very close at hand.

They stepped out to meet him.

"For Pete's sake!" he exclaimed impatiently. "What are you doing here?"

"Christie's arm is still numb," said Mora, not answering him.

"Because she *hurt* it," said Kevin positively. "We wanted to see your mysterious 'witch,' and you showed her to us. But Chris has had enough of all this magic mumbo-jumbo. It's scaring her too much. I don't want to hurt your feelings, Mora, but if you're planning on giving her any 'magic potions' at sunrise, forget it. She'll get along fine without them."

"I should think that would be up to Christie to decide," said Mora. "After all, it's her arm that's numb."

"Come on, Kevin," said Christie, pulling him by the hand. "It's almost dark, and when Mommy doesn't see us on the beach, she really will be worried."

"That's what I've been telling you," he said, leading her out of the woods.

When they reached the road, they could see Mrs. MacAlistaire at the back of their cottage, unloading the car.

"Hi, Mom!" Kevin shouted. "Wait for us!"

She waved and he started running toward her. Mora held Christie back just long enough to whisper, "Don't tell your mother about your arm, and don't let her put anything on it. Don't even wash it. It might interfere with the potion. And leave your door open—after dark."

Christie nodded, and ran down the road after her brother. Mora took the steep trail down to the beach and made her way home along the sand.

"Kevin!" Christie called, trying to catch him. "Wait for me, *please!*"

She sounded so urgent that he slowed down and let her catch up with him. "Kevin," she whispered breathlessly, "remember our oath!"

"Oath!" Kevin exclaimed in disgust. "That was the craziest—"

"That doesn't matter," Christie insisted. "We made a promise."

"Okay," her brother agreed.

"And don't tell Mommy about my arm."

"That's different."

"No it isn't. Please, Kevin. It doesn't hurt, and there's nothing she can do about it. You said yourself, it'll be fine in a day or two."

"Well—we'll see," he said. "I won't say anything, just now."

Mrs. MacAlistaire had barely started the job of unloading the car when they reached her.

"D'you know what happened to me? I fell asleep on the porch and just woke up!" she said, laughing.

"Good thing," Kevin said, "because now we're in time to help."

Their mother began handing things out of the car to them, and though Kevin said nothing about his sister's arm, he made sure that she carried nothing heavy.

"I see you made a friend and explored the headland," said Mrs. MacAlistaire. "Did you see the haunted cove?"

Kevin was so startled to hear his mother call it "haunted" that he was caught off guard, but he recovered quickly. "There was a high fence all around it with four rows of barbed wire on top," he said, managing to give her an answer without breaking his oath.

"Barbed wire!" she said, surprised. "I guess they really do want to keep everybody out."

"How did you know about it?" asked Christie.

"The real estate agent who rented us the cottage told me about it," her mother said. "Apparently the story goes back nearly one hundred years."

Christie looked at Kevin, and her eyes said, *You see, Mora wasn't making it up. It's true!*

"Did the real estate agent tell you anything about who's living there now?" Kevin asked his mother.

"Yes. Some relative of the original owner—great granddaughter, I think she said. The agent thought she'd come all the way from Europe to see her property. Slipped into town sometime last year, and then slipped out again without anyone's knowing she'd been here."

"When did she come back?" asked Christie.

"Very recently, I guess. In the meantime, she'd arranged to have the inside of the house restored by some contractor from out of town."

"And nobody around here got in to see what was going on?" asked Kevin.

"No. Apparently the fence was put up years ago, and even while the work was being done, the gates were kept locked."

"And when it was finished she slipped in again," Kevin concluded.

His mother nodded. "Just as unobtrusively as she had the first time."

"Why do you think she wants to stay there alone

in that haunted cove?" asked Christie.

"I don't know," said Mrs. MacAlistaire. "She sounds like a very mysterious lady."

Kevin didn't look at Christie. He knew what her eyes would be saying. Instead, he carried an armload of things into the house.

In the northwest, sunset comes as late as nine o'clock in early summer. It was well after nine when they returned to the cottage, so by the time they had carried everything in from the car and placed it where it belonged, it was already ten. Kevin and Christie were tired by then, and hungry, though they had stopped for dinner on the drive out to the coast.

Their mother served them tall glasses of cool milk and a special treat: large slices of blackberry pie made from the delicious big berries that grew wild in that part of the country.

Nobody had much to say. Kevin and Christie didn't dare to mention the haunted cove, and fortunately their mother seemed to have forgotten about it. She noticed that they were especially quiet, but she knew they were over-tired from the long drive and their adventure on the headland. When they had finished eating, she took over the final chores and sent them to bed.

Mora had been right: Their mother—and their father, who would join them on the weekend—would occupy the big bedroom upstairs. Kevin and Christie each had a bunk bedroom downstairs, with a bathroom and a hall stairway between, and each had a door that opened onto the lower porch.

Christie had left hers ajar, and now she couldn't wait to see what Mora had brought for her. She ran down ahead of Kevin, closed the door to her room, and snapped on the light. She had expected to find something just inside the door, but to her disappointment, she found nothing. Perhaps Mora hadn't come yet.

She could hear Kevin's footsteps on the stairs. Then he knocked softly on her door, and she heard the faint whisper of her name. She had to open the door for him—but what if he should be there when Mora came!

He slipped in quietly and closed the door behind him. "Chris," he said gently, "don't worry about what that real estate agent told Mom. Just because people say the cove is haunted doesn't mean it **is**. And besides, if they don't know anything about the woman who lives there, then they can't possibly know she's a witch."

"I guess not," she admitted.

"So forget all that stuff about invisible arrows, huh? There was nothing coming out of that flute but music."

"I know," Christie agreed, anxious to get him out of the room before Mora might arrive.

"And you don't need Mora's 'magic potion,' even if she knows how to make it—which I doubt," he declared. "So don't go over to her house at sunrise, will you?"

"No, I won't go to her house," said Christie. Whatever she decided, that much was true: She wasn't going over to Mora's house.

41

Then Kevin noticed the door to her porch. "That door's not closed," he said. Walking over to it, he opened it wide for a moment and looked outside.

Christie held her breath. If only Mora weren't walking up the stairs from the beach!

"Boy, is that surf loud!" he said.

"I love the sound of it," Christie said quickly. "That's why I like it open."

"You'll feel safer at night with it locked," he said, closing the door and slipping the bolt that locked it.

Christie waited nervously as he started back toward his own room. In her doorway, he stopped. "There's nothing to worry about, Chris," he said, "but if you should feel scared, call me."

"I will," she promised.

After he had gone, she didn't unbolt the door to the porch. The bolt was rusty, and he might hear the sound of it. She got into her pajamas and threw back the covers of her bunk bed. There, barely sticking out from under her pillow, she found the charm Mora had brought her and, with it, a note.

The charm was square and hard and heavy and it was wrapped in thick layers of white silk and tied with a white satin ribbon.

Christie unfolded the note. *Don't unwrap the charm,* it said. *Keep it under the bedding at the foot of your bed, and no evil spirit will dare to come near you. Meet me in the woods at daybreak. We have to be in the secret place early, so I can give you the magic potion just as the sun rises.   Mora.*

Quickly, Christie put the charm and the note under the bedding at the foot of her bunk, before anyone might walk in on her. She hadn't decided whether

42

she would meet Mora or not, but in case, she set the alarm and put the clock under the far end of her pillow. Then she snapped off the light switch and got into bed.

Her mind was whirling with all the strange things she had seen and heard. Her arm felt numb and the thought of it frightened her. But her feet were touching the soft layers of silk around the charm, and its meaning comforted her. She was very tired, and at last she fell asleep.

It was in the last hour of darkness before dawn that she became aware, gradually, of the distant music of a flute. At first the high weird notes seemed very far away, but slowly they came closer and closer and were louder and louder, until at last she realized the flute was right in her room.

She sat up in bed and there—just beyond the hidden charm—stood the witch in her black cloak with the golden sun and moon on her shoulders. She was holding the flute to her lips while she played the wild piercing music, but it was her face that was most terrifying. In the center of her forehead, just above her brows, there was a green eye—the same *third* eye that Christie had seen at sunset, when she had stood too long, gazing at it in horror and fascination.

Only this time she saw it clearly, almond-shaped and blazing like green fire. And while Christie stared at it, long slender arrows began to come out of the flute. They were not invisible now—they were shining like steel, and coming straight at her. Christie tried to scream, but no sound came out of her throat. With a desperate effort, she threw up her arms to ward off the fatal darts.

The next thing Christie knew, she was lying on the floor in the dark, shaking with terror. The witch was gone. She was afraid to move, for fear she'd find she'd been turned to stone. At last she moved her left arm, then her legs. She jumped up in the darkness. Her body was all right. Only her right arm was still numb. Perhaps the charm had stopped the evil arrows from touching her.

Still shivering from her fearful vision, she put on the light. Everything was exactly as it had been when she went to bed. There was no sign that the witch had been there. But of course the witch would be much too clever to leave any clues.

44

Christie was so weak from shock that she sat on the bed, and then she remembered the clock. She took it out from under the pillow. It was almost time for the alarm to go off. She pushed the lever back in so there would be no sound to disturb Kevin or her mother.

She wanted to run to her mother and tell her of her terrible experience. But her mother would think it had been a nightmare. Could it have been? Could the whole dreadful vision have been a dream? Maybe, she thought.

But she couldn't risk settling for that. If the witch with the green eye were to come again . . . No—she needed Mora and her magic potion. Swiftly, Christie jumped into her clothes, slipped out the door, and headed for their meeting place in the woods.

4

RITUAL IN THE GROVE

The night before, when Christie had found the charm in her bed along with the note from Mora, Kevin, in his room, had found something of equal interest that might have been put there by the same visitor. On a table beside his bunk, he had discovered two big magazines. To his amazement, both of them had feature articles about witchcraft, magic and sorcery.

He hadn't known what to think of Mora and her talk about her sister's book of spells and curses. He hadn't taken any of it seriously, and he certainly hadn't believed that stuff about "covens" of witches.

But this was very different. This was printed in two famous magazines, known by everyone and read all over the country. Propped up in bed, reading them, he learned about all kinds of strange and secret cults. The magazines even showed color photographs of beautiful women who admitted they were witches, and odd-looking men, surrounded by skulls and coffins and black cats, who said they practiced evil magic and put curses on people they hated.

It was pretty scary stuff to be reading around midnight, practically next door to a haunted cove. And the shocking part of it was, these weren't made-up stories—these were statements of fact about real people. One magazine said, exactly as Mora had said, that *right now* there were hundreds of "covens" of witches—and a "coven" was a sort of squad of thirteen members. Hundreds multiplied by thirteen added up to thousands!

Kevin was getting a very creepy feeling about all these peculiar people who practiced their good and evil magic, but he was also getting very sleepy. Before long, the magazines seemed too heavy to hold, his eyelids drooped, and he was sound asleep.

Shortly before daybreak, he was roused by something only half heard. It might have been a thud, as of a body falling, but the boom of the surf through his open window had already drowned out the sound.

Vaguely, he thought of Christie. She sometimes fell out of bed, especially if she were having a nightmare. He knew he ought go and see if she was all right, but trying to wake up was like trying to swim up from the bottom of a deep pool. He heard nothing more, so he let himself drift off.

It seemed only a moment later that he was disturbed again. This was a different kind of sound, but from the depths of sleep he couldn't place it. He fought to come up to the surface, to rouse himself to full wakefulness.

Christie! Whatever the two sounds had been, he'd better check on her. He dragged himself out of bed and staggered across the hall to her door.

He was coming awake now, and he remembered Mora's talk of magic at sunrise. He opened the door to Christie's room. She was gone. The door to the porch was ajar. *That* was what he'd heard the second time—the sliding of the rusty bolt.

But Christie had told him she wouldn't go to Mora's house, and it was not like her to break a promise. Suddenly he realized the ritual at sunrise might not have been at Mora's house at all. It might have been somewhere else—maybe the headland.

The thought of the headland and its dangers alarmed him. The darkness of night was already giving way to the first light of day, and he ran out on the porch. He looked up and down the beach, but there was no sign of the girls.

He ran back into Christie's room, and for the first time he noticed a piece of paper on the floor below the bunk. He picked it up and read it. So they were to meet in the woods!

He didn't even bother to look for the charm in the foot of the bed. He hurried to his room, got into his jeans and a sweat shirt, and then raced out to the porch and down the stairs to the beach. He couldn't risk waking his mother by taking the cottage stairs up to the road. He would take the steep cliff trail instead. He headed for it at a fast sprint.

As he ran, he tried to think what the secret place might be that Mora had mentioned in her note. The gap under the fence was her discovery—no one else knew about that. So perhaps it was the place over-looking the haunted cove, where they had been last night. She might have thought that to counteract the evil spell of the witch, she must perform her "magic" at the spot where the "spirit arrows" had struck Christie's arm. At least it was the only secret place he knew of. He'd have to start with that.

He was out of breath when he reached the road at the top of the cliff, but he kept running. If only he could catch them before they tried to go under the fence! They had come so close to disaster last night that the thought of Christie's trying to crawl under, handicapped by her injured arm, was frightening to him.

He reached the woods and turned in. The girls were nowhere in sight. Gasping for breath, he ran on desperately, dodging between the dark tree trunks.

After her experience last night, it was hard to believe that she'd risk going under the fence again— unless her fear of the witch was even more terrifying.

Christie was very imaginative—his mother had explained that to him. You could tell it by the way she looked at the clouds in the sky and saw a hundred shapes no one else saw. It was the same with tall grasses blowing in the wind, and with designs the sea made in the sand. Everybody else walked on them, blotting them out with their feet, but Christie was careful never to step on them. She bent over them by the hour, seeing all sorts of beautiful things. And if you told her the beginning of a story, she could imagine a dozen different endings. So it was easy to understand how she could have been impressed by Mora's story of the invisible arrows coming out of the flute, and believed that the witch had *almost* succeeded in turning her to stone.

Maybe her arm had felt more numb in the night. It could have, if she'd been lying on it while she slept. And then there was that thud he'd heard.

Perhaps she had had a horrible nightmare about the witch and fallen out of bed.

Whatever happened, she must have been very frightened, he thought, to get up in the dark and come alone to meet Mora in the woods. She must have felt a terrible need for the comfort of Mora's "magic."

He had been following along the fence where Mora had led them last night. Now he reached the gap beneath it. There was nothing to tell him whether or not the girls had been there.

He edged cautiously toward the rim of the cliff. He was almost afraid to look down to the rocks below. When he did, he saw, gratefully, that Christie and Mora were not there.

He pulled himself through the gap under the fence and crawled up the slope. At the top, he could see the spot where Christie had stood last night when she sighted the pillars of stone that had looked like the young couple.

The girls weren't there. His guess had been wrong. This was not the "secret place" of Mora's note. But still it might be somewhere in the woods on this side of the fence.

He walked cautiously through the trees, searching for some glimpse of Christie and Mora, listening for the sound of their voices. But he saw only the forest, still gloomy in the early light, and heard only the morning breeze sighing through the pines.

He couldn't resist the temptation to stop and peer down at the cove. The old house looked dark and cold in the shadow of the cliff, and on the front porch he saw the two white seagulls standing watch.

For just a moment, he let his mind imagine that they were two young men, bewitched.

Then he said aloud, "That's crazy!" He was turning to go when he glimpsed something that stopped him cold. Far out in the waters of the cove there was a sudden violent motion. He ran to where he could get a better view.

What he saw was astounding: An immense whirlpool was spinning in from the sea. Its racing circles whirled around with incredible speed, getting wider and wider on the outside, while at its center they spun down into a vortex so big it could swallow a boat. The wild thing seemed to be whirling in toward the beach, and he fled. Without caution, he sped down the slope, swung himself under the fence, and raced back into the shelter of the woods.

What was the story of the curse that haunted the cove? he wondered. He'd have to find out.

But now he had to find Christie. He looked up through the treetops and saw a white cloud beginning to turn pink. That meant it was almost sunrise. If he didn't find Christie before then, she would drink the potion.

He shivered, thinking of what might be in it. He had read of the horrible ingredients witch doctors used for their kind of magic—stuff so awful it could make Christie sick.

He began to run into a part of the woods where he hadn't been before. But they grew thicker, and he slowed down, realizing he might have a better chance of hearing the girls than seeing them. Mora, if she were performing her ritual, would probably start with saying some kind of spell.

51

The cloud was getting brighter, and he knew he had only moments left. He felt as if he must run against time. Instead, he forced himself to walk quietly, listening. But it was a fragrance that gave him his first clue. It was not the normal smell of the forest. It was something different, like perfume. Incense! That's what it was. He recognized the smell because his mother burned it sometimes. Mora was burning incense now, and she was near at hand.

He stood still, trying to tell from which direction the fragrance came. And then, over the soughing of

the wind in the pines, he heard a chanting. The sound was as hard to trace as the incense. Both seemed to move around him with the morning breeze.

He walked in a circle, and as he came to a dense thicket of undergrowth, the chanting became louder. The words were strange—he couldn't understand them—but he was sure it was Mora saying her spell.

He ran around the thicket, trying to find a way to get in, but the branches were so interlaced they had formed a strong green wall. He couldn't break through without an axe. His only chance would be to go under.

Searching along the ground, he spotted a crawl hole that was like a small tunnel. He got down on his hands and knees and began to snake his way into it.

Suddenly the tunnel widened, and he saw ahead of him an open glade. It was a beautiful place, with the branches of tall trees arching over it like an arbor. Above them, the clouds were a bright crimson. In the center of the glade a large boulder pointed up toward the sky, and on its tip he saw the rising smoke of the incense.

He couldn't see the girls, but the sound of the chanting ended. Then from behind the rock, Mora rose and stood with a shining glass goblet held in her two hands. In it was a white liquid.

Kevin watched, spellbound, as if someone had taken away his power of speech, when Christie rose to receive it. Mora spoke two strange words while Christie took the goblet from her. As she lifted it to her lips and drank the potion, the sun rose.

5

A SURPRISING STRANGER

Christie had drunk the potion right before Kevin's eyes, and he had let her do it! *Why?* he wondered. He'd searched the headland to find her and protect her from Mora's "magic"; there had been an instant before she drank it when he could have shouted "Stop!" and she would have heard him. Yet he had lain in the thicket and let it happen. It was as if Mora's spell had reached out to silence him.

That was impossible, he told himself. Mora couldn't really make a spell, much less a potion that was "magic." But denying her powers didn't relieve his anxiety. Whatever she had made, Christie had drunk it—a whole goblet full.

He watched his sister's face intently for some reaction. If she turned pale, it would mean the stuff was going to make her sick. He'd seen that familiar warning sign before. But he saw no clue to an oncoming illness now. In the sunrise light, Christie's face seemed to glow, as if she felt greatly relieved and happy.

He wondered if her arm was still numb, or whether in the excitement of the ritual she'd forgotten all about it. Perhaps that was the answer, he thought. She had been terrified that the witch's spell was turning her arm to stone. But apparently Mora had put on such an impressive performance that now Christie believed in her powers. And that belief had overcome her fear. Whatever Mora had done, he wouldn't question it if it had worked and Christie felt safe again.

But he'd better get out of here, he realized, before the girls discovered him. The ceremony was supposed to be performed in secret. Christie might even think the power of the spell had been weakened if she knew that he'd seen any part of it. It would be stupid to destroy her faith in it now.

He couldn't risk turning around in the thicket. The grove was so quiet that the slightest crackling of a twig would betray him. He'd have to back out. It had been hard enough to crawl forward on his hands and knees, while Mora was covering any sound he might make with her chanting. But now she was silent. In fact, she and Christie were out of sight behind the rock, but they might come around it at any second.

He began to work his way backward through the crawl hole, feeling like an inch-worm moving in reverse. He didn't dare look back over his shoulder to see what treacherous branch might be lying in the path of his toes, knees or elbows, for merely by turning his head he might snap off a twig. Hardly daring to breathe, he edged back inches at a time, wondering how the little tunnel could possibly be so long, and then at last he was out of it, and in the clear.

He got to his feet and, still moving cautiously, walked away from the thicket and back toward the tip of the headland. He hadn't gone far when he heard the muffled sound of Christie's and Mora's voices. That meant they were coming out. He raced for a sheltering stand of firs and hemlocks and hid behind the swollen base of a lone red cedar. When the girls crawled out of the little tunnel, he would pretend that he was just returning from the witch's cove.

Christie was the first to emerge, and Mora followed, dragging after her a sack that, Kevin guessed, must contain the objects she had used in her ritual. He waited until they were well away from the thicket and heading through the woods toward the road. Then he shouted "Hey, Chris! Mora!" and started running after them.

They stopped and looked back at him in shock and amazement, and as he came close, he knew by the odd, secretive look in their eyes that they feared he had witnessed their ceremony.

"Where have you been?" he asked quickly, to ease their fears. "I've been looking everywhere. I even went over to the witch's cove."

"You mean you came from there *just now*?" Mora demanded, her gray eyes smoky with suspicion.

"And fast!" said Kevin, slipping easily over the matter of when he had come. "I scuttled under that fence like a lizard. Do you know what I saw?"

"What?" asked Christie breathlessly, her fears about the ritual forgotten.

"A whirlpool with a hole in the middle of it big enough to swallow a boat!"

"A whirlpool!" Mora's face paled. If he'd said he'd seen the devil himself, Kevin thought, she couldn't have looked more stunned.

"Have you ever seen one?" he asked.

"No," she said apprehensively, "but a whirlpool is part of the curse."

"You mean last night's curse, when you said invisible arrows came out of the flute?" Christie asked in alarm.

"I mean the first curse made almost one hundred years ago," Mora said, her voice husky with awe. "The whirlpool came then, and maybe last night this witch cast a spell with her flute that made it come again. If she did, we'd better get out of here. There's no telling what will happen next."

Clutching her sack of ritual objects to her chest, she started to run. "Come on," she whispered urgently, "while the magic is still working to protect us!"

It took all Christie had to keep pace with her, and Kevin followed behind his sister. Mora didn't stop till she'd reached the safety of the open road.

While the girls paused for breath, Kevin asked, "What could happen?"

"Who knows?" Mora gasped. "It might start all over again—dead men walking on the beach—"

"Dead men!" Christie shivered with horror.

"Look, Mora," Kevin said, his voice knife-sharp, "you keep talking about that old curse and scaring Chris with a lot of bits and pieces that don't make any sense. It's time you either shut up about it or told us the whole story."

His tone antagonized Mora, and she was about to

57

snap back at him, but the piercing look in Kevin's brown eyes stopped her.

"Well?" he demanded firmly.

"Okay," she agreed a bit sulkily, "but I can't tell you now. I've got to get home before my mother wakes up."

"When, then?" asked Kevin, pinning her down.

"This afternoon," she promised. "I'll meet you on the beach."

When Helen MacAlistaire woke up, Kevin and Christie had already made their bunk beds and put their rooms in order. Christie had hidden the heavy charm, wrapped in its silk covering, under her pillow, and Kevin had secreted the magazines with their information about witchcraft in the bunk above his own.

Neither of them mentioned their daybreak adventures on the headland to their mother, and she assumed that they were up early because they were eager to get out onto the beach. But even after she had served them a hearty breakfast and the dishes were done, it was still a bit cool for swimming or sunbathing on the sand. Instead, the three of them voted to go into the village to do the marketing for the day and buy skim boards for Kevin and Christie.

It was a very small town, stretching for a few blocks along the two sides of the main highway, and they had no trouble finding the place they were looking for. Huge green letters painted on the side wall of a barnlike building informed every passerby that this was O'Flaherty's General Store, Terence O'Flaherty, Proprietor. In fact, Kevin thought, Mr.

O'Flaherty's store might well have been a barn, sometime in the past. And when they got inside, he saw why it needed to be so big.

O'Flaherty's carried almost everything a person could need: clothing and hardware, meat and groceries, and yes, skim boards, too, for skimming along the shallow water on the beach. While their mother shopped for groceries, Kevin and Christie picked out their boards, a red one for him, a blue one for her. When they took them up to the counter beside the cash register, they were confronted by a gentleman who had to be Terence O'Flaherty himself.

He was a solid figure of a man, big-shouldered and thick-bodied, with a grizzled beard and moustache. On his head he wore a visored cap, but Kevin was most impressed with his pipe. It was an amber yellow, with a stem that curved like an S turned backwards, and it had a large bowl.

Noting Kevin's interest, the man said genially, "It's a calabash pipe, made from a bottle gourd that grows in the tropics, and a cooler, more friendly pipe no man ever smoked."

"Are you Mr. O'Flaherty?" Kevin asked.

"That I am!" said Mr. O'Flaherty, the pipe still anchored in the corner of his mouth. "And who might you be, my lad?"

"I'm Kevin MacAlistaire and this is my sister, Christie, and we're staying out on Cliff Loop Road."

"In the seventh cottage," Christie volunteered.

"In the seventh, h-m-m," said Mr. O'Flaherty thoughtfully. "I'm wondering, what have you heard about your neighbor in the eighth house?"

"There isn't any eighth—" Christie started to say.

But Kevin cut in. "You mean the house in the haunted cove."

"Ah, I see you *have* heard. But do you know what happened to Jimmy Cooper, my delivery boy, one day when he was leaving an order of groceries on the back stoop, there?"

"No, sir," said Kevin.

Mr. O'Flaherty leaned toward them and spoke in a low, conspiratorial voice. "He fell and broke his leg, that's what. And all because of the frightening thing he saw through the window!"

"What did he see?" asked Christie nervously.

"He saw the lady of the house, herself—and d'you know what he claimed? That she had a green eye— an *extra* one, mind you—right in the middle of her forehead."

"Holy smoke!" Kevin exclaimed.

"And what's more, Jimmy swore if his brother hadn't been with him, driving the truck, she'd have come out and found him helpless there, and put a spell on him."

The horror of Christie's vision of that third eye took hold of her again. Mr. O'Flaherty saw that her face had paled and her hands were trembling.

He took his pipe out of his mouth. "Now, Christie, lass," he said gently, "you know that boy had to be lying. A green-eyed woman, that I've seen, and mighty handsome she was, too. But an extra eye, be it green or red or yellow, that *nobody* has seen!"

"I've seen it!" Christie said, the words spilling out before she realized it.

61

"You have, now!" exclaimed Mr. O'Flaherty, raising his bushy eyebrows in astonishment. "And when did you see it, may I ask?"

"Last night," Christie managed to whisper, already regretting that she'd let it slip out.

Kevin was staring at her in amazement. "What are you talking about, Chris? When did you see the green eye?"

Christie wished desperately that she'd never mentioned it. She couldn't tell them she'd seen the green eye from the top of the headland. "In the middle of the night," she said, knowing they'd think she'd been dreaming.

"Then you *were* having a nightmare," said Kevin, "and the thud I heard was you falling out of bed."

Christie nodded, anxious to drop the subject.

"A nightmare! Now that's different," said Mr. O'Flaherty. "I can tell you, Christie, I've had nightmares that would make a three-eyed woman a comforting sight, by comparison. But wide awake in broad daylight—I'd be willing to bet that's something neither you nor I will ever see."

I saw it in daylight, Christie thought, but she didn't say so.

Mr. O'Flaherty was smiling at Christie reassuringly, his lips parted in a wide grin that showed nearly all of his teeth, and Kevin could hardly believe what he saw.

Mr. O'Flaherty caught his look. "Ah! Now you've seen something else almost as peculiar," he said, chuckling.

Kevin couldn't take his eyes off the teeth. They

seemed to be double, as if Terence O'Flaherty had two rows, one behind the other.

"And they're all my own," O'Flaherty insisted. "I grew them myself, every one. What d'you think of that, now?"

"What made them grow that way?" asked Kevin, still fascinated by the phenomenon.

Mr. O'Flaherty leaned over the counter confidentially. "Just between you and me," he said, "I think my parents forgot to put out a saucer of milk for the leprechauns on the night I was born, and those little Irish fairies took their spite out on me." He gave Kevin and Christie a knowing wink. "But they gave me a gift to make up for it," he said. "Watch now, and I'll show you."

He straightened up and put his pipe in his mouth. Then he drew on it deeply. When he exhaled the smoke came not out of his nose—but out of his *ears*.

"Hey, that's great!" Kevin exclaimed enthusiastically. "Can you do it again?"

"Sure and I can. A hundred times in a row if I want to."

Again he drew on the calabash pipe and sent the smoke floating out of his ears.

"Did you ever see anybody else who could do that?" he asked Christie.

"No, never," she said, wide-eyed with wonder.

"Well, then, your neighbor over there in the haunted cove isn't the only odd one in town, is she? In fact, Terence O'Flaherty's peculiarities are on display in broad daylight for anybody to see, and that's the only kind to believe in. You remember that, Christie—just believe in what you can see for yourself, with the sun shining."

On the drive back to the cottage, Christie thought about Mr. O'Flaherty. He was warm and kind, and she knew he had seen how frightened she was and wanted to reassure her with his talk about his teeth and the leprechauns and the gift they had given him. It comforted her to know he was there, big and strong and funny, and already their friend.

But neither he nor Kevin knew that what she had seen in the dark of night, she had first seen at sunset, when she could see as clearly as the delivery boy. Perhaps only she knew that Jimmy Cooper hadn't been lying.

Even with the prospect of skidding along at the water's edge with their skim boards and a picnic lunch on the beach, she could hardly wait for the hours to pass until it would be afternoon and Mora would come.

At length lunch was over and Helen MacAlistaire went back up to the cottage. They were a musical family, and though Kevin and Christie had been excused from practice during their holiday, their mother had brought her violin. She would be playing it now for at least two hours. They would be alone with Mora.

Christie watched impatiently for her to come while Kevin listened to his favorite birthday gift, a pocket-sized transistor radio. He was idly shifting from station to station when he came upon a news bulletin. Christie wasn't listening. Her thoughts were intent on Mora, her nerves taut with waiting.

"Chris—did you hear that?" Kevin demanded suddenly.

"No, what?" she asked absently.

"There was a bank robbery at Brookport less than an hour ago. The robbers shot it out with the guard, but they made a getaway with forty thousand dollars! The guard thinks he winged one of them—a young fellow with a black beard."

"Oh," said Christie, not really taking it in.

"The getaway car was a white station wagon," said Kevin, "and they were reported heading into the mountains."

Christie didn't answer. She had been watching the lower story of the fifth house, and now she saw the door of Mora's room opening.

"You know, Brookport's not even fifty miles south of us," Kevin said thoughtfully. "Maybe heading into the mountains was just a trick. Wouldn't it be something if they made a semi-circle and came out here?"

His words didn't even register on his sister. "Here comes Mora," she said. "Now at last we'll find out about the first curse."

6

THE BLACK CURSE OF THEODORA

Kevin shut off his radio, and the three of them sat in a tight little huddle, Mora in her skirt and blouse of many colors, and Kevin and Christie in their T-shirts and shorts, one on each side of her.

"There's so much to tell I hardly know where to begin," Mora sighed. "I guess I'd better start with Theodora."

"Who was she?" Christie asked eagerly.

Mora looked around to make sure no one was within earshot. "The first witch," she confided, "but in the beginning nobody knew it. I don't think she even knew it herself. She didn't live here then." Mora's gray eyes lifted to the headland and the glimpse of the cove beyond. "The story really begins before her father bought that cove and built the house."

"Where were they then?" Kevin asked.

"Somewhere in northern California, in the mother lode country."

"You mean back in the gold-mining days?" Kevin was intrigued.

Mora nodded. "Her father was a sea captain, but he left his ship to prospect for gold. I guess it was a bad time for Theodora and her mother. He didn't

have any luck, and they were terribly poor. If Theodora had been pretty, she might have managed to get a husband. But she was very plain, and skinny as a pencil."

"Maybe she was half-starved," said Christie, already feeling a sympathy for the unfortunate girl.

"Maybe," said Mora. "Anyway, she must have been desperate, because that's when she first started to learn about witchcraft."

"How could she learn about that in a mining camp?" asked Kevin, in surprise.

"There was a sailor named Chut who had come to the camp with her father—a man from the South Pacific," Mora said. "Theodora had known him when he was on her father's ship. He'd told her stories about witch doctors and magic men on his island, about their spells and potions and curses. Only she wasn't interested in curses, then. She wanted to put a love spell on a man."

"And Chut knew how?" asked Christie.

"He said he did. It happened his mother was a magic woman on his island, and her specialty was to make a love perfume. When he was a boy, he'd helped her collect all the secret ingredients, and he remembered what they were."

"And he told Theodora?"

"I think he made it for her. Anyway," said Mora, her voice hushed with awe, "the perfume was so powerful that if a girl could touch the man she wanted with a drop of it, he would fall in love with her even if he'd hated her before that."

"Did it work?" asked Kevin bluntly.

"She never used it," said Mora, "because it was then that her father struck gold. He got hold of an old worked-out mine, dug deeper, and struck a ledge of new ore. It was a big bonanza, and suddenly he was very rich. He bought that whole cove because he wanted to live beside the sea." Mora indicated the haunted cove with her glance. "And then he built that big house, and Theodora had so many suitors she didn't need any magic perfume. *Or so she thought!*" Mora added with chilling emphasis.

"What happened?" asked Christie, in concern.

"Theodora fell in love with one of her suitors. His name was Stash, and he was young and very handsome. He'd drifted into the mining camp when she lived there, but she was so thrilled when he asked her to marry him that she forgot he'd never paid any attention to her before her father struck gold."

"He was just after her money," Kevin surmised.

"Of course," said Mora, "and then just a week before the wedding an odd thing happened. He was prospecting, too, and he struck gold himself."

"So he didn't need Theodora's money any more," Kevin concluded.

"And she'd forgotten to put the love perfume on him," said Christie, with distress.

"That's the awful part of it," Mora agreed. "She'd had it all the time, but she'd never thought to use it."

"It wouldn't have worked," Kevin declared positively. "You can't tell me a drop of some crazy perfume would change how a man felt."

"It worked on Chut's island," Mora insisted.

"Well, that's not here," said Kevin, "and anyway she didn't try it, so we'll never know."

"We know what her curse did," declared Mora.

"Was it Stash she put the curse on?" asked Christie.

"Yes. Her friend Chut heard Stash was running out on her and told her about it. He was leaving by boat from the little river port on the other side of that far promontory—the one that juts out on the north end of the haunted cove. The port's still there, and the old lighthouse near the jetty. That's where the fishing boats are moored now. Chut found out

Stash was sailing that evening at sunset for San Francisco."

"He told her that, too?"

Mora nodded. "He knew Stash was no good, but he felt sorry for Theodora because she wanted him. He thought maybe she could get down to the boat before it sailed and put a drop of the perfume on him. Then he'd fall in love with her and stay here."

"And she didn't make it?" asked Christie anxiously.

"She didn't try," Mora declared. "When she found out he'd never loved her at all but only wanted her money, her love for him turned to hate. She didn't want to put the perfume on him—she wanted to curse him, instead. So she asked Chut to teach her a death curse."

"A death curse!" Christie exclaimed in dismay. "Did Chut do it?"

"No, he refused—or at least that's what he told the police."

"The police? How did they get into it?" asked Kevin.

"You'll find out," Mora promised, "but that was years later."

"If Chut refused," said Christie, "how could Theodora put a curse on Stash by herself?"

"Partly because she remembered some of the stories Chut had told her about his island. One of them had been about a woman who put a curse on some men who were sailing away on a ship. She remembered that the woman had made clay images of the men and the ship, and then she'd taken them

70

down to the shore and said a death curse over them and thrown them into the water."

"What happened to the ship and the men she was cursing?" asked Christie.

"The ship sank and the men were all drowned."

"So I suppose Theodora made a clay image of Stash and his ship," said Kevin.

"That's right," said Mora. "She sent Chut away, and then she took a knife and went down onto the slope under that big front porch where nobody could see her, and cut the images out of the cliff. When she'd finished she hid them in her dress and walked way out onto the top of that far promontory, just as we walked out on this one last night."

She indicated the headland nearby, where they had stood together when they saw the woman playing her flute.

"From the top of that promontory," Mora went on, "she could see the river and the port and the ship preparing to sail. When it began to move away from the pier, she stuck pins into the clay image of the man. And then she started to say the curse—"

"Wait a minute," Kevin cut in skeptically. "How could she say it when she didn't even know it?"

"Because her hate was so strong that the evil words she said were as powerful as any death curse, and they worked for her," Mora insisted positively. "She stood on the tip of the promontory and demanded that the ship would sink to the bottom of the ocean and Stash would drown. Then she threw the clay images of the boat and the man over the cliff into the sea."

71

"What happened then?" Christie asked, her voice hushed with apprehension.

"The ship sailed slowly down the river and out beyond the headland into the open sea. Suddenly, as it turned south, a strong wind rose and sent a giant whirlpool spinning in toward Theodora's cove."

"Just like the one I saw this morning," said Kevin, impressed in spite of himself.

"I told you it was part of the curse," Mora reminded him. "Theodora saw it coming and screamed for it to catch the ship and swallow it, and that's exactly what happened. The ship was caught in the whirlpool and sucked down until it disappeared beneath the ocean."

"The one I saw was big enough to do it," Kevin admitted.

"What happened to all the men on the ship?" Christie asked in alarm.

"When they saw their ship was going down, they all jumped from its deck and tried to swim, but the whirlpool was too strong for them and they were sucked under, too. All except Stash. He was a powerful swimmer and somehow he reached the outer circle—and then as suddenly as it had come, the whirlpool was gone, and he was swimming toward the shore of Theodora's cove."

"You mean her curse drowned all those innocent men, and the guilty one survived?" asked Christie.

"Almost," said Mora. "The wind was still strong and the sea was rough, but Stash was fighting for his life and he reached the shore and started to drag himself up the stairs into the cavern."

"Theodora must have been fit to be tied," Kevin

72

declared, "with her whole curse working out the wrong way."

"She was," Mora admitted. "Stash was getting up into the cavern out of reach of the sea, and it must have been then that she gave her soul to the evil powers forever in exchange for a great wave. Because the wave came—greater than any that had ever come into the cove. And it rushed up the stairs and filled the cavern and Stash was drowned!"

There was a moment of shocked silence, and then Kevin asked, "Is he the one that's buried in the urn?"

"Yes," Mora admitted, "but nobody knew it for years and years. Theodora got Chut to help her bury him in a shallow grave until she could have the urn made. It was a huge thing, over six feet tall, and no one ever guessed it was really a coffin."

"Except Chut," said Kevin. "I suppose he was the one who put Stash into it."

"He had to," whispered Mora, paling at the thought. "Chut found the place where Theodora had cut the clay images out of the cliff, and he realized she'd put the curse on Stash and the ship. After that, he knew she had the powers of an evil witch, and he didn't dare refuse her anything. So he sealed Stash's body inside the urn, and it has stood in the cavern ever since."

Christie shivered with horror. "There's something I don't understand," she said. "If Theodora hated him so, why did she want him there?"

"Out of revenge," said Mora. "Because he tried to get away, she wanted to keep him as her prisoner forever."

From Mora's house, they heard her mother's voice

calling her name.

"But Theodora forgot one thing," Mora went on, ignoring the call. "She forgot that even a witch can't keep ghosts buried if they choose to walk at night."

"You mean the ghost of Stash walked out of his urn?" asked Kevin.

The voice of Mora's mother became insistent.

"I've got to go now," Mora said. "My mother is catering a big dinner tomorrow night, and there are special gourmet things I have to help her pack. But I've only told you half of the story. The death curse was just the beginning. The most awful part is what happened to Theodora."

"When can you tell us about that?" asked Christie, eager, yet dreading to hear it.

"If I can get away, I'll meet you at sunset on the headland. But in the meantime, you could walk past the house and listen for the organ."

"What organ?" Kevin demanded.

"Theodora's," said Mora. "Sometimes you can hear her ghost touching the keys. It's entirely different from the sound of living hands."

"Have you heard it?" asked Christie.

Mora nodded. "It's very strange and eerie. Walk past and listen carefully."

7

A FACE IN THE FOG

Kevin and Christie gathered up their beach towels, skim boards and chairs and carried them up to the house. A fog was rolling in, white and silent, over the sea. It hung so close to the water that from the height of their porch it seemed like a cloud floating in space below them. It chilled the air, and they went inside to put on jeans and sweaters.

From upstairs came the singing tones of their mother's violin in a brilliant cadenza that was like a lively dance. Christie wanted to linger and listen, but Kevin was anxious to reach the house of the witch to listen for the ghostly organ music of Theodora.

As they walked along the road, the fog was rising, blotting out the shape of the headland and stretching its long white fingers into the dark greenness of the forest. They could barely see the beach now, and the ocean beyond it was shrouded in mist. Even the breakers seemed muffled and far away.

The whole mood of the day had changed, and as they approached the old house, the fog flowed up over the cliffs and enveloped them in a filmy curtain that cut off the last bit of sunlight. The trees became pale and blurred, and the house with its turrets and chimneys wavered before them as though it were suspended in the unstable air.

"Let's go back," Christie whispered, shivering.

"Why?" Kevin demanded.

"Don't you feel them?" his sister asked.

"Feel who?"

"The ghosts," said Christie, her hushed voice barely audible. "I can feel the cold of them all around us. It's not just Theodora—it's those others. Any minute they'll reach out and touch us. Please, Kevin, let's go back."

"Oh, come on, Chris," said Kevin impatiently. "You're getting as kooky as Mora. The cold you feel is the fog, not ghosts. I'll turn on my radio and it'll snap you back into the real world." He took it out of his pocket and turned the switch.

"Not here!" said Christie apprehensively.

But almost instantly a newscast blared out, loud and clear.

"Shut it off!" Christie pleaded. "The witch will hear us!"

"Sh-h," Kevin hissed softly, turning the volume down low. "It's about the bank robbers."

He held the little radio close to his ear, listening intently. Christie waited, not hearing the muffled words, while the feeling of cold persisted, penetrating her body in spite of her warm sweater. It was not just the fog, she was sure of that. She'd been in much thicker fogs before and never felt this strange sensation. It had nothing to do with weather. It was something apart from this world, as if some invisible presence had reached inside her and touched her heart with ice.

"Did you hear that, Chris?" Kevin whispered as she shut off the radio. "The robbers have abandoned their station wagon in the mountains behind Brookport. The police think they've stolen another car and maybe kidnapped the driver, but so far they haven't any leads. Gosh," he added thoughtfully, "those thieves may just have made a clean getaway. I wonder which way they *are* headed."

"They could drive right up this street and kidnap *us*, and in this fog nobody would see them," said Christie, hoping to alarm her brother. "Let's go home!"

"What would they want with us?" asked Kevin, totally unimpressed. "If they've already got a car and a hostage, two kids would just be a nuisance. Come on, I want to get a good look at the old house, and listen for the organ."

Christie had no choice but to follow. She didn't want to go back alone in the fog, and certainly she didn't want to stand and wait in this place, with its feeling of invading cold. Besides, she was as curious as Kevin about the ghostly music.

They walked noiselessly in their sneakers along the high chain-link fence that separated the house and its grounds from the road. When they reached the driveway, they found, surprisingly, that the big car gate was unlocked.

"That's so Jimmy Cooper can get down there with the groceries and spy on the witch and her green eye," Kevin said teasingly.

77

Christie ignored him. She had already spotted the four steps up to the back stoop, and the small window above it. It would have been through that window that Jimmy had seen the witch, and then he must have turned and fallen down those steps. That would have been how he broke his leg, she thought.

The driveway slanted down to what must once have been a handsome stable. At some time, perhaps in the recent renovation, part of it had been converted into a garage, but the heavy swinging doors were partly open, and they could see that there was no car inside.

"Why should she buy a car when she can ride her broom?" said Kevin, still needling his sister.

"Shut up," she hissed back at him, "and listen for the organ."

Kevin grinned and stood beside her, listening intently. As he waited for the eerie sound, he studied the structure of the old house. The two top floors rose up from the same level as the garage. Obviously the lower floor was built into the slope of the hillside, below.

But there was something odd about the place, and suddenly he realized what it was. Windows! There weren't any—or almost none—on the whole rear of the house. Only that one small window above the back stoop looked out from the middle level onto what had been the stable courtyard. And on the top floor, another small window, perhaps at the head of a stairway, looked down over the courtyard and driveway and out toward the street. All the rest was solid wall.

It gave the place a secretive feeling and reminded Kevin of the small openings in the turrets of castles that were used, in the old days, for gun emplacements to defend them against attack. He wondered if Theodora's father had built the house that way in the first place or whether, after the terrible disaster that followed her curse, they had covered over the windows to shut out the people of the town.

The lady who lived there now, whether she was a witch or not, must be as secretive as the house, he thought, for over both little windows the shades were drawn. Nobody could see in—or out.

"Do you hear anything?" Christie whispered.

"No, nothing—but look, the fog's lifting," said Kevin, noticing that the white curtain of mist around them was opening up, and here and there patches of sunlight were breaking through. "Let's follow the road to the edge of the bluff, so we can see the river and the port."

Christie agreed readily. For now, at least, the ghostly musician was silent, and she was glad to escape from the area of the old house and the icy chill that seemed to reach out from it to touch her with invisible hands.

Kevin's mind was already racing ahead to something that intrigued him more than the view from the bluff, but he knew he'd have to work up to it gradually or Christie would never consent to go with him. They walked to where the road turned inland abruptly toward the town, and stood high above the river while the fog drifted erratically, giving them glimpses of the old harbor and the fishing boats tied up at the docks. Then it closed in over the port and opened up down-river, so that they saw the outline of the abandoned lighthouse anchored to a table-topped rock on the opposite bank.

Kevin spotted a trail that led along the edge of the bluff toward the sea, and he was quick to take advantage of it.

"Let's follow this trail to where we can look down on the lighthouse and the jetties," he said, hoping Christie wouldn't realize that he was leading her out onto the northern promontory of the haunted cove. From its tip, Theodora had screamed her death curse, and that would be the last place his sister would want to go.

"I bet the fishing is great from those jetties," said Kevin, running ahead before Christie had time to question him.

He maintained his lead, shouting back comments to keep her attention fixed on the lighthouse and jetties. They had covered half the length of the headland when the trail came to an end, and Christie caught up with him.

Below them, the waters of the smooth-flowing river crested and foamed as they collided with the breakers that rushed in between the long rock-arms of the jetties. Directly across from them stood the old lighthouse, the windows of its squat white dwelling broken, its tall tower empty and dark.

"It looks so lonely," said Christie wistfully, "like a person that's been left behind."

Like Theodora! she thought, and for the first time she realized that this was Theodora's promontory, that somewhere out near its tip she had stood as

Stash sailed down the river leaving her behind. If only she hadn't cursed him, Christie thought. If only she'd put the love perfume on him, instead.

"I wonder how much candlepower its lantern had," Kevin said.

"H–m?" murmured Christie.

"The lantern in the lighthouse," Kevin said. "They must have used kerosene to keep it burning in the old days. I'll bet its beam went out ten or fifteen miles and saved lots of ships."

"It couldn't save Stash's," said Christie.

"Nothing could save his ship," said Kevin. "It was—" He stopped short. To his amazement, he had almost said, "It was cursed." But he didn't believe in the power of curses—or did he? He covered quickly by saying, "It was the whirlpool that took it down."

"But what caused the whirlpool?" asked Christie, her eyes searching his.

"I've been thinking about that," said Kevin. "It might have been the wind, or maybe the way the two headlands jut out makes currents that bounce back on each other and start it whirling. Or it could be caused by the river flowing out, or the shape of the sea bottom. There has to be some practical reason."

"If there is, why don't whirlpools happen all the time?"

"Well, maybe they do," said Kevin, convincing himself. "Who's there to tell? I saw one this morning."

Christie's eyes told him she *wasn't* convinced. "I don't want to think about it," she said. "Let's go

81

back." She turned toward the trail, but Kevin grasped her arm.

"No, wait, Chris. I want to go up on top and see if I can get a look at the cove from this side."

"I don't want to," said Christie, trying to pull free.

"Please, Chris," Kevin pleaded urgently. "We won't go far, I promise. It's just like the other side. There's a high fence up there in the woods. I saw it from the trail."

"And you'll want to crawl under it," Christie protested. "Well, I *don't* want to. I'm going back."

"Oh, come on, Chris. I won't go under the fence— I probably won't even have a chance. But maybe there'll be a spot where I can look between the trees and see how the lady gets out to her rock. It could be she rows out in a boat and climbs up a stairs we can't see from the other side."

"I don't think she needs a rowboat or stairs," said Christie.

"Well, I do!" Kevin insisted. "And if you'll come with me, I bet I can prove I'm right. There's nothing to be afraid of, Chris. It's just woods, like the other side, and in broad daylight. Even the fog is going out."

It was hard to resist her brother's pleas, and Christie surrendered and climbed, with his help, up the slope. There was no trail now, and the terrain was steeper and more rugged than that of the headland at the other end of the cove. The forest seemed thicker, too, the great stands of hemlock and fir taller, and the wind-twisted pines on the rim more dense.

When at last they had struggled up to reach the fence, they found it was exactly like the other one, six feet high with barbed wire on top, and no space beneath it for Kevin to crawl under. Beyond the fence, the land continued to rise, sloping up to a heavily wooded summit, and there was no place where anyone could get a view of the cove.

Kevin ran eagerly along the outside and Christie hurried after him, trying to keep him in sight as he darted in and out between the trunks of the trees. But either they were running into the fog, or it was rolling back over them, for he disappeared in the mist and she found herself alone.

There was nothing to do but follow blindly, though she knew that he was leading her out toward the head of the promontory. Her only guide now was the fence, and she kept as close to it as the underbrush permitted, for the fog was getting thicker with every step.

As she moved forward carefully, trying to avoid collision with the dark shapes of the trees, they seemed to be closing in on her like tall guardsmen, their circle growing tighter around her until she could see no way of escape. The icy chill she had felt as she stood near the old house was penetrating her body again, and she stopped, feeling even more strongly than before that she was near an alien presence.

She wanted to call out Kevin's name, but she felt a pressure on her throat, as if something were cutting off the sound. The dark guardsmen were leaning down over her, crowding her to the fence. The fog seemed suffocating, and she knew she couldn't bear to move one step closer to the tip of the headland where Theodora had stood, cursing the clay images as she hurled them over the cliff.

Even here, Theodora seemed frighteningly close —and suddenly Chris understood why. No more than six feet away from her stood a marble headstone, and beyond it, two more. Only the fence separated her from the private family cemetery. If Stash was buried in the urn, then these must be the graves of Theodora and her parents. The first headstone was a life-sized figure of a robed woman, and then Christie saw the wings folded gently behind her shoulders. An angel! Was she the guardian of Theodora's grave?

Christie had to know. She pressed up to the chain-link barrier and peered through the mist. The name cut into the marble base was Erikson—not Theodora, but Mary. That must have been her mother.

Beside the angel stood a tall oblong column topped by a figurehead such as might have been on the prow of a ship. The Captain's ship. She could barely make out the weatherbeaten lettering: Captain Jonas Erikson.

The third headstone stood beyond them, farther out toward the sea. It was a massive but severe marble cross. The fog was swirling around it like a shroud, and Christie strained to make out the name on the base.

It was not Erikson. The letters seemed to waver in the mist and she spelled them out slowly: J-e-l-i-n-e-k. Who was that? Had Theodora married, or was this the grave of someone else?

It couldn't be! Christie thought. The presence she had felt, so cold and lonely, so desolate, had to be Theodora's. The sensation was so strong she could almost see her.

85

She leaned into the fence, peering beyond the surname to the first name. One by one, she made out the letters and pieced them together. They added up to *Theodora*. So it *was* she who lay beneath that cross! Theodora Jelinek. She must have married, after all. Yet she lay alone beyond the graves of her parents with no husband, no child beside her.

"I've only told you half of the story," Mora had said. "The death curse was just the beginning. The most awful part is what happened to Theodora."

Suddenly, Christie's heart jolted with terror. Above the center of the cross, a ghostly face appeared. It was a white wraith in the mist, yet she knew it was not the face of a woman but of a man, young and dark and bearded. As she stared at it in horror, the fog closed down over the cross and the face was gone.

Christie found her voice and screamed, "Kevin— where are you? Kevin! Help me!"

After a nerve-wracking silence, Kevin answered, and came running back out of the mist. "What's the matter?" he shouted in alarm as he approached.

"I saw him!" Christie sobbed.

"Saw who?"

"Stash!"

"Stash? What are you talking about?" Kevin demanded.

"I saw his ghost," Christie cried. "He was standing behind her cross."

"Whose cross?" he asked in bafflement.

"Theodora's. The marble cross on her grave."

"I don't see any marble cross," declared Kevin, looking through the fence.

"Right there!" Christie insisted, pointing to where it had been. But though she could see the gravestones of the Captain and his wife, the cross beyond was completely obliterated by the fog.

"You imagined it," said Kevin gently. "The fog's playing tricks on your eyes."

"The fog's hiding it now, but it was there, and so was he," Christie declared vehemently. "I saw them both and I wasn't imagining!"

"Okay, okay," said Kevin, putting a comforting arm around his sister. "In this fog, *anything* could be there. It's closing in so fast we can't see more than a yard ahead, now. We'll have to follow the fence back to the road. I'll lead and you stay right with me!"

"You bet I will!" said Christie.

They moved slowly and cautiously, the fog cold and moist on their faces as they threaded their way between the dark, vaporous shapes of the trees. Following closely on Kevin's heels, Christie was haunted by the face she had seen in the fog.

It *must* have been the ghost of Stash, she thought. He had looked like the young man Mora had described. And he, more than any of the others who died there, would have been drawn to Theodora's grave and to the place where she had cursed him.

But something else made her sure it was he—something she had seen in his face. Though he was only a ghost now, and she had seen him but dimly, yet the look was still there—a look of menace. She wondered why Theodora had not seen it in the beginning and been warned. She, herself, Christie thought, would have known better than to trust him.

And then a frightening idea occurred to her: did ghosts have a power over living people? Could he come up behind her, silence her with a ghostly hand, and draw her back into the white cloud of mist without Kevin's even knowing she was gone? Could he, if he chose, push her over the cliff and into the sea?

An icy chill shook Christie's body, and she ran to catch up with Kevin and grasp his hand tightly. Guided by the fence, they completed the long, slow trek through the woods and came, at last, to the road. Ahead of them a shape loomed up, so blurred that they were almost upon it before they saw that it was a camper parked at the curb. Vaguely, they could make out a shadowy figure sitting behind the wheel.

Common sense told them he was a man, trapped as they had been by the fog, and too wise to try to drive until it lifted. But the camper and its occupant gave Christie an uneasy feeling, and she was glad Kevin was willing to hurry with her toward home.

8

THE GHOST
THAT WALKED

At dinner that night, Christie was still haunted by the face she had seen behind the marble cross. She wanted very much to talk to her mother about it, but the memory of the oath she and Kevin had taken made her hesitate. Still, she thought, what they had promised Mora was that they wouldn't tell what they had seen *last night*. That concerned crawling under the fence and seeing the witch on her rock. But this was of a different place, a different time, and it had nothing to do with the witch and her flute.

They were lingering over a delicious raspberry custard when Christie said suddenly, "Mommy, do you believe in ghosts?"

"Believe in them?" said her mother thoughtfully. "Well, I've never actually seen one, if that's what you mean, but stories of ghosts go back as far as there have been people to tell them."

"I don't mean made-up stories—"

"I don't either, Christie. I mean that there have always been some people who have seen ghosts, or sincerely believed they have."

"But they haven't really, have they, Mom?" asked Kevin. "Weren't they all just ignorant or superstitious people?"

"Far from it, Kevin," said his mother. "Some, of course, have been ignorant or superstitious, but many have been highly educated, brilliant people."

"Well, then 'sensitive,' like you say about Chris," Kevin suggested.

"Yes, certainly some of them have been more sensitive than the average person," his mother agreed.

"And *imagining*, like Chris, today?" said Kevin.

"I wasn't imagining," Christie declared positively. "I saw him behind the marble cross."

"Wait a minute, you're way ahead of me!" Mrs. MacAlistaire exclaimed. "Are you saying you saw a ghost today, Christie?"

"I really did, Mommy. His face just suddenly appeared above the cross."

"You realize, of course, that I don't know what cross you're talking about," said her mother humorously.

Swiftly, Christie filled in the essential facts of their walk out onto the headland, her separation from Kevin, and her discovery of the private family cemetery.

"It was the fog, Mom, the way it was floating all around, that made Chris think she saw a ghost," Kevin cut in. "I was right there, and I didn't see a thing."

"That's true," Christie retorted. "You didn't even see the marble cross, but it was there! Before the fog hid it, I even read the name on it: Theodora Jelinek."

"Theodora Jelinek!" exclaimed Kevin in surprise.

"And I wouldn't make that up," Christie insisted. "I've never even heard of anyone named Jelinek."

"All right, so maybe there was a cross," Kevin conceded. "But that doesn't mean there was a ghost."

"And it doesn't mean there *wasn't!*" said Mrs. Mac-Alistaire surprisingly. "Kevin is right about one thing, Christie—the fog could have created the illusion of a gray, ghost-like figure."

"But he wasn't all gray—not really," Christie interrupted, "because I saw the dark look of his hair and beard."

"You imagined that part," said Kevin confidently.

"Not necessarily," said his mother. "There's something *you* must realize, Kevin: The fact that you didn't see the ghost doesn't mean that Christie didn't. Even if you'd been there at the exact moment when she saw it, it might not have been visible to you."

"Why not?"

"There's no simple answer to that, Kevin. For the last hundred years or so, many very intelligent men and women have been making a serious study of ghosts and hauntings."

"They have?" Kevin was amazed.

"Yes," said his mother, "and they've found that if, say, ten people were in a room or garden when a ghost appeared, perhaps eight of them saw it in exactly the same way. But the other two saw nothing."

"So you mean the ghost could really have been there, even if I didn't see it?"

"According to their evidence, yes," his mother admitted. "The fact is, we don't know. Nobody really knows. We're just beginning to learn a little about many things that can't be proven by ordinary scientific methods."

"Mom," said Kevin thoughtfully, "if Chris did see a ghost, could he be a man who died there long ago, like almost one hundred years?"

"I don't think the length of time has much to do with it," said his mother. "We've all heard about old houses and castles that have been haunted for many, many years. It's more a matter of *how* the man died, of what *happened* there. If there was some intensely emotional act connected with his death—"

"There was," Kevin cut in excitedly.

"Then perhaps that would be what holds him there," said his mother. "Or it could be that the emotions connected with his death were so strong that they charged the whole atmosphere of the place—"

"Like with electricity?" asked Kevin.

"Something like that. And Christie just happened to tune in."

"Golly, I wish I could tune in," said Kevin.

"Tuning in doesn't necessarily involve seeing a ghost," his mother explained. "You may be tuning in to the atmosphere of a place when you feel a sudden change of mood from happiness to sadness or loneliness."

"I felt a terrible coldness when we stood near the old house," said Christie.

"I didn't feel anything but the fog," said Kevin candidly.

"Out by the cemetery, I felt the presence of Theodora before I ever saw the face of the man," said Christie. "It was a different feeling—very sad and lonely. But the face behind the tombstone was frightening, as if he might want to harm me. Mommy, could a ghost draw a person back to the edge of the cliff—and push him over?"

"Were you afraid of that?" asked her mother.

"Sort of," admitted Christie.

"Then the only danger was in your fear of him," said Mrs. MacAlistaire. "No ghost, dead one hundred years, could harm you, unless in your imagination you *believed* he could."

"You mean," said Kevin, "that if Chris imagined he was trying to draw her back and push her over, she might have walked back to the edge herself, and slipped over?"

"Yes, such things have happened to people, out of sheer terror, because they saw ghosts—or thought they did. Remember, Christie, you may have imagined the ghost, as well as the danger," her mother reminded her. "We have no way of knowing whether you really saw a face in the fog, or felt a presence."

"But I could have," said Christie.

"Yes, you could have," her mother admitted. "But I'd rather you and Kevin didn't go out on that headland again without your father. In a lonely woods like that, there could be 'presences' that weren't at all ghostly."

Kevin and Christie both thought of the shadowy figure in the camper, but they didn't mention him. In the morning, their mother would drive inland to the city. Their father was head of the music department in one of the high schools, and he was on a committee that was sponsoring a benefit concert. They would be staying at the beach cottage alone while

93

their mother stayed over in town to attend the concert. Then on the following morning their parents would drive back together. After that, their father would be with them for the summer, and they could go anywhere.

But now they could hardly wait for their meeting with Mora. The smothering blanket of fog had dissipated long since, and the headland and sea were clear again. Well before sunset, they hurried up the road. The camper was gone, and they slipped into the edge of the woods, as they had the night before, but Mora was not there.

"Maybe she meant for us to meet her out where we saw the witch," said Kevin.

"Do you think we ought to?" said Christie doubtfully. "Mommy just said—"

"She wasn't talking about this headland," Kevin told her confidently. "This one isn't nearly as lonely. Besides, it's practically next door to our house, and we've already been here twice."

And both times have been awful, Christie thought, remembering the near disaster at the fence, and the double terror of the witch with her green eye, at sunset and in the night at the foot of her bed. This morning there had been the whirlpool, and their running in fear lest, as Mora had said, it should all begin over again with dead men walking on the beach—

Kevin cut into her thoughts. "You won't fall this time. "I've brought a rope," he said, opening his windbreaker to show her a sturdy length of it coiled several times around his waist. "And if you're worried about the witch, she can't do you any harm. It's like Mom said, it's all in your mind. And if you want

94

to believe in evil magic, then you've got to believe in good magic, too, haven't you, because Mora's magic cured your arm."

Christie was silent, remembering the beauty of the sunrise in the sacred grove.

"Well, didn't it?" Kevin demanded. "I've noticed you haven't said anything about its being numb, and you've used it the same as you always do."

"Yes," said Christie. "She cured it."

"Then we've got nothing to be afraid of," Kevin insisted. "Come on, before we miss everything."

Reassured, Christie ran with him through the woods. They were earlier than they had been the night before, and the low sun was still slanting through the forest, warming it with a rose-red glow. In this light, Christie thought, it seemed safer, more as it had at sunrise.

When they reached the fence, Kevin looped one end of the rope around his sister's waist and tied the other to the chain links, so that she couldn't possibly slide down the chasm. Then he swung under and pulled her safely through after him.

They climbed the slope, crawling up the last few feet to the crest, as Mora had done. When they peered over the top she was nowhere in sight, but the haunted cove lay below them, the weird shapes of its huge black rocks looking just as strange and eerie as they had remembered. And then they heard again the high notes of the flute.

"She's out there!" said Kevin excitedly. "Let's crawl down to where we can see her."

"But don't let her see you!" Christie warned in a whisper.

They crept carefully down toward the trees at the

rim of the precipice, and flattened themselves out
on the pine needles beneath the low-swung branches.
From their lookout, everything seemed to be as it
had been last night: The witch was standing out at
sea on her rock-tower wearing her black cape, with
its gold disks reflecting the last light of the sun; her
two guards, the white sea gulls, were perched on each
side of her; and the sea lions were splashing the
water around the rock into a creamy foam.

Only the sound of her flute was different. The
wind that had risen out of the west to blow the fog
away was carrying the music to them clearly, and
there were no sharp, piercing notes. Instead, it was
sweet and mellow, with a magic quality such as they
had never heard before from a flute. The melody
was unfamiliar, as if the musician were composing
it as she played, ranging up a full three octaves in a
way that lifted Christie's heart. She listened in fascination until Mora's voice, behind her, broke the
spell.

"I'd have been here sooner, but I had to finish

something," she said mysteriously, indicating the wooden cigar box she was holding in her right arm.

"Finish what?" asked Kevin.

"You'll find out," she said, crouching down beside them. "It's a surprise."

"Chris has a surprise for you," said Kevin impressively.

"What?" Mora demanded.

"Well, I'm not exactly sure about all of it," said Christie hesitantly.

"Of course you're sure!" Kevin insisted. "Tell her, Chris!"

"All right. I saw Stash," said Christie.

"Stash!" Mora stared at her in amazement.

"I mean his ghost," Christie amended.

"Where?" Mora asked sharply.

"Behind the tombstone on Theodora's grave," said Christie. "His face was lean, and he had dark hair and a dark beard."

"That's right," said Mora, her gray eyes wide, her voice hushed with awe.

"Of course it was very foggy, and I could have imagined I saw him," Christie admitted honestly, "but one thing I am sure of: Theodora's buried out there at the tip of that other promontory under a marble cross—"

"Is she?" Kevin cut in.

"Yes," Mora said.

"And she married a man named Jelinek."

"Yes, she did. He was her father's lawyer."

Christie shot a look at her brother that meant, "I told you so!" but she didn't say it aloud. After all, he had wanted Mora to know about the ghost.

"I went out on the promontory once and saw the cemetery through the fence," said Mora. "Maybe I didn't see Stash because it was a bright sunny day, but I can believe his ghost is still there on her grave, because he haunted her day and night until finally she went with him."

"Went with him!" Kevin exclaimed. "What do you mean?"

"Wait!" Christie interrupted. "Don't skip around. I want to hear the story from where you left off—after Chut buried Stash in the urn."

"That's when the haunting began. Gradually, the bodies of all the men who had drowned in the whirlpool were washed up on her cove, and their ghosts began to walk."

Christie looked down beneath the branches of the pine, imagining the awful scene. Even the music of the flute seemed melancholy now, as if the musician were tuning in to the eerie memory of the past.

"Theodora made Chut keep lighted torches burning in the cavern to drive the ghosts away, but even though she was a witch, she had no power to stop them," said Mora. "She could see their filmy white forms on the beach at night and hear their wailing. She never dared go down to the shore again, even in the daytime, and at night she played the pipe organ as loud as she could to drown out the ghostly cries in the cavern. The townspeople walking along the road used to hear her playing 'Nearer My God To Thee' until the house thundered with the sound."

"How did her father and mother put up with that?" asked the practical-minded Kevin.

"They weren't there long. They both died of a

mysterious disease within a month of the day she put the death curse on Stash," said Mora. "You saw their graves out on the point."

Christie nodded.

"After that, she was alone, except for Chut. He was afraid of her powers, so he stayed on as her servant and lived out in the stable. It was then, when she was all alone at night, that the ghost of Stash began coming up out of the cavern and into the house."

"How awful!" Christie breathed.

"Why didn't she leave?" asked Kevin.

"Because she was bound by her dreadful secret," said Mora.

"You mean because she'd buried Stash in the urn?"

"Yes, and because of her curse. I think the evil powers that made it work kept her there. She couldn't break away from them or the ghosts, and she was terrified of living alone."

"So she married Mr. Jelinek," Kevin concluded.

"He was the only one she ever saw, except Chut," said Mora. "She never went out of the house, so he came there because he was in charge of all her money and her property."

"And she must have been loaded," said Kevin.

"Yes, she was very rich," Mora agreed, "but even so, I think she must have put some of the love perfume on him, to make sure she'd get him—and keep him."

"Did she keep him?"

"Yes, until Stash—" Mora broke off. "But that was later. First, she married Josef Jelinek."

"What was he like?" asked Christie.

"He was older than she was—about fifteen years—but he was a nice man, and I guess because of the perfume he really loved her. Anyway, he stayed with her and for a while the ghost of Stash stopped coming into the house. But after her baby was born—"

"She had a baby?" asked Christie in surprise.

"A girl," said Mora, "and they named her Theodora."

"And after she was born, Stash came back into the house?"

"Yes. Theodora thought he was trying to get the baby. She was so terrified she confessed everything to her husband—all about her death curse and the ship sinking and all the men drowning."

"What did he think of that?" asked Kevin.

"He told her it was all in her mind," said Mora. "That she couldn't have put a curse on the ship, that whirlpools occur where the floor of the ocean is uneven, and its coming and swallowing the ship when she was saying her curse was just a coincidence."

"Did she believe him?" asked Christie.

"She couldn't because she knew that even if the whirlpool had just 'happened,' it was she who caused the great wave that rushed up into the cavern and got Stash. And besides, she saw his ghost come into the house every night."

"Did her husband ever see him?" asked Kevin.

"No, he told her the ghost was in her mind, too—that because she felt *guilty*, she imagined he was there. But nothing he could say made any difference."

"What did she do?" asked Christie.

"Well, for a while she saw Stash's ghost only in

the living room. He never came into the bedroom, though she was sure he was just outside the door. So she put the baby's crib right beside her bed and stayed awake all night to watch over it."

"Poor thing," said Christie sympathetically. "How could she?"

"She couldn't, for very long," said Mora. "She was so exhausted she was getting weaker and wilder all the time. Finally, even though he didn't believe in the ghost, her husband took turns with her, watching over the baby half the night just to humor her."

"Why didn't he get rid of the urn with Stash's bones in it?" asked Kevin.

"He didn't know about that," Mora explained. "I think she was afraid to tell him for fear he would get rid of it and something terrible would happen. But finally one night, in her desperation, she did tell him—and that was the night the ghost of Stash walked into the bedroom!"

9

A PERILOUS
EXPERIMENT

The black-caped woman was still out on her rock, but Kevin was so absorbed in Mora's story that he had forgotten her, and even Christie was only vaguely aware of the silvery sweet sound of her flute in the background.

"What happened after his ghost came into the bedroom?" asked Kevin.

"Nobody knows exactly," said Mora. "It was Theodora's turn to watch over the baby, so Josef was sound asleep. All of a sudden he heard the baby screaming in terror. He jumped out of bed, only half awake, and took her up in his arms—and then he saw that the bedroom door was open and his wife was gone. He walked out into the living room with the baby, who was still screaming, but his wife wasn't there. And then, because it was a moonlit night, he saw her outside on the porch, and she was starting down the stairway into the cavern."

"Oh, no!" Christie murmured.

"Josef ran back to the bedroom and put the baby into her crib, and then he went down after his wife. It was a stormy night, and the wind had blown out all but one of the torches in the cavern. He could barely see Theodora as she passed the burial urn and disappeared from view. He ran down the stairs and when he got to the bottom, he saw her walking across the beach toward the water, and for the first time he saw the ghost of Stash."

"He did!" Kevin exclaimed in amazement.

"Yes," said Mora. "The ghost was leading her into the sea and she was following him like a sleepwalker."

"Didn't Josef try to stop them?" asked Christie.

"He shouted her name, but she walked right into the water as if she didn't hear him. Josef plunged in after them, but the breakers were huge and when he got past them, the ghost of Stash had vanished and Theodora had gone under. He jack-knifed and managed to find her, but by the time he got her back to shore it was too late. He couldn't revive her."

"So she drowned just like Stash and all the men on the ship she had cursed," said Christie thoughtfully.

"I guess the ghost of Stash got his revenge," said Kevin. "If there really *was* a ghost."

"Of course there was," Mora insisted. "Not only did Josef see him, but so did the baby!"

"How do you know that?" Kevin demanded.

"Because she screamed every time her father tried to take her into the bedroom. She must have seen Stash and remembered him, because she never let Josef take her there again. So after he and Chut had told the police all they could, Josef closed up the house and went abroad with little Theodora, and they never returned."

"And nobody's ever lived in the house since—until now?" asked Kevin.

"No," said Mora. "The whole story was published

in the paper, and no one would buy it or rent it because of the curse and the ghosts and the dead man's bones in the urn. Who'd want to live there, except a witch?"

The three of them peered down at the mysterious woman on the rock.

"She's the great granddaughter of the first one," said Mora, "and I've heard her name's Theodora, too."

As she spoke, the sound of three piercing notes from the flute hit them with the sharpness of arrows.

"She's casting a spell," Mora whispered fearfully.

"It's not for us," said Kevin. "She's looking out to sea."

"That doesn't make any difference," said Mora. "She could know we're here. She could know what I've been saying."

Again the three notes came shrilling out of the flute.

Mora's face was pale, but Kevin said, "It sounds to me as if she's calling something."

"She could be calling her coven of witches," said Mora nervously. "That twisted tree on her rock is probably the coven tree."

"What's that?" whispered Christie.

"It marks the place where the thirteen witches have their meetings and cast their evil spells. If they come while we're here, something terrible will happen to us."

Again the high, thin notes pierced the air, and this time there were seven, just as there had been last night when Christie's arm had gone numb.

"Come on, let's get out of here," Mora whispered frantically. "And don't dare raise your heads. *Crawl!*"

Moving awkwardly with the cigar box gripped tightly in her hand, she began to creep up the slope. Christie followed her, looking back desperately at Kevin, who was staying behind under the tree.

"Come on, Kevin!" she pleaded urgently.

"You go on," he said. "I'm going to stay and see who comes."

"If it's the coven, they'll bewitch you!" Mora hissed in a final warning.

"Kevin, please!" Christie begged. "You won't see anything if they turn you to stone."

But Kevin ignored her, lingering under the tree to view the cove below.

Mora reached the crest and carefully edged herself over it. "Hurry, Christie," she urged, "before it's too late."

"But I can't leave Kevin. He's my brother!" Christie protested, reaching the crest and looking back at him. He was lying calmly under the pine branches. From the cove came another series of seven high weird notes.

"If we can reach the sacred grove before the witches come, I think I can save him," Mora whispered. "But it won't take them long to get here. We'll have to run like crazy."

With the aid of the rope Kevin had left attached to the fence, they swung safely under it and sped through the forest. When they reached the little tunnel in the thicket, they crawled through into the open glade and ran to the place behind the big

105

boulder where Mora had conducted her secret ceremony.

Near its base there was a flat slab of rock some two feet high. At sunrise, this had been the altar on which she placed her ritual objects and mixed her magic potion. Now she knelt and placed the cigar box on it.

"I haven't time for the whole ceremony," she said, gasping for breath. "If I'm going to save Kevin, I have to put a spell on her before her coven gets here."

She opened the box and inside, to Christie's amazement, there lay a doll made of clay dressed exactly like the witch. She had on a little cape fashioned out of black velvet with shiny gold seals on each shoulder for the emblems of sun and moon, and in her crudely-

shaped hands she held a tiny spear of bamboo with holes punched in it, to represent her flute.

"I've been working on her for days, and it looks as if I finished her just in time," said Mora. "If that's the coven tree, then she's the queen of the coven, and the most powerful witch of them all. I'll have to use the strongest curse I know to overcome her, and you can help me."

"Curse!" Christie exclaimed in dismay. "But that's evil magic."

"She's an evil witch," said Mora. "It'll take evil magic to stop her."

"But I thought you wanted to be a good witch," said Christie.

"I do," Mora insisted. "But I'm trying to save Kevin, and maybe even *us*, and the only way I can overpower an evil witch is with her own kind of magic."

She took a handful of sharp black-headed pins out of her pocket and gave them to Christie. "Here —take these. We've got to hurry."

"No!" she protested. "Whatever it is, I won't do it!"

"There's no time to argue," said Mora harshly. "Don't you want to save Kevin?"

"I don't know that she'll harm him. I don't even know for sure that she's a witch," Christie cried defiantly, "and I won't take part in any evil magic, not ever!"

"Then I'll do it. Give me the pins!" Mora commanded.

"No. I won't let you do it either," said Christie positively. "If you put a curse on her, maybe you'll be haunted just like the first Theodora. The witch could haunt you just as Stash did her, until you were led into the sea."

"I hadn't thought about that," said Mora slowly. "I just wanted to stop her from doing evil. But maybe I'd better not put a death curse on her. I've got another idea."

"What is it?" asked Christie doubtfully.

"We won't hurt her," said Mora. "I'll just take away her flute and break it so she can't cast any spells with it." She took the tiny bamboo flute out of the doll's hands, broke it in two, and threw it away. "And then I'll nail her in her box."

"Nail her in? Why?"

"We have to do something to protect Kevin. It'll be just like locking her up, so she can't get out to harm anybody."

Mora took some small nails out of a pocket and with a stone began to hammer them in around the edges of the cigar box. As she hammered, she said, "Evil witch, great granddaughter of Theodora Jelinek, with these nails I lock you in and make you my prisoner, so that you won't be free to harm Kevin or us or anybody."

When she had finished, the box was sealed tight.

"But now she can't breathe," said Christie.

"A clay image doesn't have to breathe," said Mora impatiently. "She's just a symbol. We haven't done anything to torture her or destroy her. I won't say any curses over her."

"You promise?" demanded Christie.

"I promise," said Mora. "It'll just be an experiment between us two, and we won't tell anybody.

Without any curse or magic words, it probably won't work. But tomorrow night at sunset—" she broke off, with annoyance. "Oh, shoot, I won't be here tomorrow. I have to help my mother serve that dinner. But you and Kevin could come and see."

"What are we supposed to see?" asked Christie.

"If she's out on her rock with her flute. If she isn't, then maybe our experiment will have worked, and she'll be shut up in her house or somewhere," said Mora. "I wish I could be here to see. There's even a minus tide before sunset, and we could go around the headland and into her cove."

"Would you dare?" asked Christie, in surprise.

"Maybe," said Mora. "If she turned out to be my prisoner, then she couldn't come out until I decided to let her."

"But you wouldn't know until you got there," Christie reminded her.

"No," Mora admitted, "and if it didn't work, it could be very dangerous. We could end up like that young couple—just three rocks standing in the sea."

Somewhere outside the thicket, they heard Kevin calling their names.

"He's safe!" Christie cried with relief.

"Maybe I saved him by locking her up," said Mora. "Come on, let's go out before he finds us. And remember, don't tell him anything."

Together, they ran across the glade and crawled into the cramped tunnel of the thicket, with Mora in the lead, carefully protecting the box with its secret contents. A few moments later, they had joined Kevin.

"What happened out there?" Mora asked him.

"Plenty," said Kevin slyly, "but I'm not going to tell you runaways."

"That's not very nice," said his sister reprovingly. "Mora worked a spell to protect you, and that could be the only reason you're safe."

"I doubt it," said Kevin, grinning. "What's the surprise in the box?"

"We're not going to tell you!" declared Christie.

"You saw something out there," said Mora. "I can tell."

"That's right, I did," Kevin agreed.

"I won't ask you what, but just tell me one thing: How many were there?"

"I couldn't really count them," said Kevin, surprised by her question. "Why? What difference does it make?"

"I'll tell you what difference," said Mora. "Witches can take any form they choose, and if twelve of anything came to the rock, then they were the coven."

"H–m–m," said Kevin. "I never thought of that."

10   MINUS TIDE

That night, in his room, Kevin pulled the magazines down from the place where he had hidden them in the upper bunk. Then he got into bed and began to read them again, searching for more information about covens.

He knew they were squads of thirteen. That would mean the witch on her rock, plus twelve more who came when she called. He was sure that she *had* called with the high, thin notes of her flute, and he had seen what had come, but it hadn't occurred to him that they might be witches. Nor had he had time to count them. Thinking back, he realized that there could have been twelve.

What bothered him was Mora's statement: "Witches can take any form they choose, and if twelve of anything came to the rock, then they were the coven." Could that possibly be true? Could witches take any form they chose?

He skimmed through the long columns about American witches and wizards and all the kooky things they did, but there was nothing to prove that any of their spells and curses worked.

And then he found an article about the magic men of islands in the South Pacific—islands like the one

111

Chut had come from. And magic women, too, like Chut's mother. Their secrets, it said, had been handed down from generation to generation, going far, far back. They could make people die with their magic, though they didn't do it anymore. And they could make them live when they were so sick there was no other cure. And just as Mora had said, they could make a love perfume that worked. There were people who claimed to have seen all these things happen.

The powers of the island men seemed much more impressive, Kevin thought. But even though he read all about their secret medicines and frenzied dances and chants and prayers, he didn't find the answer to his question. Perhaps somewhere in all those long pages there was something that said witches could take any form they chose, but if so, Kevin fell asleep before he came upon it.

In the morning after breakfast, Mrs. MacAlistaire showed Kevin and Christie the food she had prepared for them: cold chicken sandwiches with potato salad for lunch, a fine pot roast with vegetables that need only to be heated for dinner, and an ample supply of milk and fresh fruit, bread and cereals. There was, in fact, far more than they could possibly eat before she got back from the city.

Though they were welcome to go in with her to attend the concert, she understood why they both preferred to stay at the beach. She had asked the neighbors to keep an eye on them, but she knew from experience that they could take care of themselves. They were free to enjoy picnicking, wading and gliding along on their skim boards until sunset. After that, they were to come in, keep the doors locked, and during the night leave on some lights upstairs and down. Not that anything had ever happened to anyone in the little row of seven cottages, but it was wiser to take care.

Only when she was ready to leave did she make two special requests: "Promise me you won't go in swimming while I'm gone," she said. "The surf can be dangerous. And I'd rather you didn't go out alone onto those headlands, either one of them," she added. "Sometimes a forest can be dangerous, too."

The request about swimming Kevin and Christie had expected, but the one about the headlands was a blow. Each of them had a particular reason for wanting to go to the spot above the haunted cove at sunset.

Their mother saw the disappointment in their faces. "Oh, now, it's not all that bad," she said lightly. "You can hold out until tomorrow. Your father and I will leave early in the morning to escape the heat. We may even be here by noon. Then we can all swim in the sea and invade the headlands together."

They couldn't go to their secret place, Christie thought, because they'd promised Mora never to tell anyone about it. Maybe that would mean they could never go there again, or see the mysterious witch.

Then Christie remembered the minus tide. That would be far more dangerous than their mother could even guess, but she wasn't asking for any promises about that.

"Sure," Kevin was saying. "That'll be great."

"Then you will give me your promise?" their mother asked, searching Kevin's brown eyes and then Christie's blue ones.

"You bet," said Kevin. "No swimming, no forests. We promise."

"We promise," said Christie, a little less positively, because of what was in her mind.

Her mother was still searching her eyes, sensing that there was something in them, unspoken, withheld. But she let it pass.

"Good!" she said. "Then I won't have to worry, because you've never broken a promise to be before, and I know you won't now."

When she had kissed them and hugged them both, she got into the car and started the motor. "And don't go hobnobbing with any ghosts," she called out cheerily. "Wait for me!" Then she pulled out into the road and drove along the Cliff Loop. Kevin and Christie waved at her until she made the turn toward the highway, waved back, and disappeared from view.

"I sure hated to promise about the headland," said Kevin.

"Um-hm," said Christie absently, still thinking about the minus tide.

Kevin took a good look at his sister. "You've got something on your mind," he said. "I can tell."

"So could Mommy," said Christie. "I was afraid she'd ask me what it was."

"Well, what is it?"

"I can't tell you," said Christie firmly, turning away from her brother and going into the house.

"Oh, come on now, Chris, why not?" asked Kevin, following her inside.

"Because if I'm the only one who knows about it, we won't do it, but if you know—" She broke off, realizing she'd already said too much.

"But if I know, we will!" said Kevin.

"We might," Christie admitted.

"Then why shouldn't we?" Kevin demanded. "It isn't something we made a promise about."

"No, not exactly, but—"

"But what?"

"Well, Mommy didn't want us to do anything dangerous."

"And this is?"

"Yes, but she didn't know about it."

"If you're not going to tell me, I'm going to guess," Kevin declared.

"I'm not going to tell you," said Christie, "because I don't think we should do it."

She walked over to the big bay window and stood watching the breakers rolling up onto the beach. In spite of herself, her eyes were drawn to the headland. The tide was high now, and the sea was hurling itself against the cliff, but later it would be possible to pass between the rock and the water, or so Mora had said. Christie wanted as much as Kevin to go there; even more, she thought, because he didn't know what she knew—he didn't know about the secret experiment.

Kevin was mulling things over in his mind, trying to guess. "It isn't anything we promised not to do," he said thoughtfully, "but it's dangerous. "What's dangerous, besides swimming—or maybe being alone in the forest? And what would we *want* to do besides swim or go out onto the headland? I can't even think—"

At the mention of the headland, Christie turned quickly away from it to look at the beach, but not quite quickly enough. Kevin had caught the motion, and it had given him the clue.

"The headland!" he said, coming to stand beside her at the window. "It's got something to do with the headland—but *not* our promise."

He stared at it, watching the breakers send up great fountains of foam as they struck the rock. "The tide's sure high," he said without thinking. And then suddenly, he got it. "The tide's very high!" he said excitedly. "So high that later it will be very *low*! That's it, isn't it, Chris? This afternoon there'll be a minus tide and we won't have to go out onto the headland—we can *walk around it*, on the beach!"

Christie didn't answer, but her eyes betrayed her.

"I guessed it, I guessed it!" Kevin shouted jubilantly. "And you're right: Now that I know, we *will* go!"

"We shouldn't," Christie protested. "It *is* dangerous, and you know it."

"Not if we time ourselves with the tide," said Kevin. "We'll go just as soon as it's low enough to let us get around the headland, and we'll come back before it gets high again. That way we'll be perfectly safe."

"Maybe from the tide," said Christie, "but not from the witch. If she should see us, she could blow a spell on her flute and turn us to stone."

"I don't believe that," said Kevin.

"I saw it happen," Christie declared. "I saw the young couple—"

"You saw the young couple," Kevin cut in, "and later you saw two tall rocks, but you didn't *see anything* happen."

"The rocks looked just like them," Christie insisted. "You saw them yourself."

"I didn't see much," said Kevin. "Mora was so hysterical, telling us to fall flat, that I flopped."

"I've never told you *all* I saw," said Christie, remembering the green eye, "but it was enough to make me believe everything."

"What did you see?" Kevin challenged. "The green eye? That was just a nightmare."

"No it wasn't," said Christie. "I saw it at sunset when she turned toward me. I'd never even heard about Jimmy Cooper, but he wasn't lying. It was there just the way he said—right in the middle of her forehead."

"Yeah?"

With the delivery boy to back her up, and even his mother conceding that Christie might have seen a ghost behind the tombstone, Kevin was more impressed than he cared to admit. He wondered, now, if what he had seen *could* have been the coven.

"If the tide is right," he said, "maybe we can get around the headland before she comes out to her rock, and then get back after she goes in."

Christie thought about the clay image that Mora had nailed in the box, wondering if the witch would come out at all.

"Come on," Kevin was saying, "let's run down to Mora's and borrow her tide table."

While Kevin stood out on the porch of Mora's

house studying the schedule of high and low tides, Mora drew Christie into her room.

"You didn't tell him about our experiment, did you?" she whispered.

"No, but he wants to go anyway," said Christie.

"Did he tell you what he saw last night?"

"I didn't ask him. I was afraid he'd ask me about the box."

"Whatever he saw," said Mora, "I'll bet it was her coven."

"If it was," said Christie, "I don't want to go into her cove."

"Oh, they won't be there tonight," said Mora. "They won't come unless she calls them."

"Maybe she will."

"No, she won't. I fixed that."

"You didn't put a curse on her?" asked Christie in alarm. "You promised you wouldn't!"

"No, not exactly a curse," Mora whispered. "But I had to put a stronger spell on her. When I thought about it, I realized she could still have been out on her rock when I nailed her in the box. That could mean she'd be stuck out there where she could see us or call her coven or anything. We didn't want that."

"No," Christie admitted.

"We wanted her locked in the house," said Mora. "So after I got home, I took out the nails and said a different spell—one I found in my sister's book. Then I nailed her in again, and said it a second time. I bet she won't get out now until I let her."

"But you will, later?" asked Christie, in concern.

"Maybe," said Mora casually. "We'll see what happens."

"Chris! Mora!" Kevin was calling from the porch.

"Don't tell him anything," Mora whispered as they went outside.

Christie didn't answer, and Mora hadn't noticed that she had never made her any promise about the clay image and the box.

"I think I've got it figured out," said Kevin. "Do you know exactly when the witch comes out on her rock?"

"About half an hour before sunset," said Mora, "and she stays out until the last light is fading."

"Then it's going to work just the way I said," he declared excitedly. "We'll be able to get into the cove before she comes out, and then, if we watch carefully, we can make it back after she goes in."

"I know something that will help," said Mora. "On the other side, there's a little clump of trees just above the high tide line. I've seen it from the top. When you get around the headland, run as fast as you can and duck under it. She won't be able to see you there."

Why should we have to run and duck, if the witch isn't going to come out on her rock? Christie wondered. Perhaps, after all, Mora wasn't as sure of her spell as she pretended to be.

The day was bright and clear, but though it was perfect for lunch on the beach and wading and skimming, Kevin and Christie could think of nothing but the minus tide. It was nearly seven hours away, and the time passed so slowly it seemed forever.

They went in early to heat the pot roast. It was one of their favorite dishes, but they hardly knew what they were eating. They finished their after-dinner chores quickly and went out on the porch to check the tide.

"It's going out," said Kevin. "It won't be long now."

A fresh breeze was rising out of the northwest, and with the sun already slanting down toward the horizon, the air was chill.

"It's getting cold," said Christie. "I'm going to put on jeans and a sweater."

"Wear something that won't show up against the cliff," said Kevin. "And a cap. If the witch should be out there, she'd be sure to spot your golden hair, especially with the sun on it."

Christie got into tan Levi's and pulled a matching turtleneck over her head. Then, standing in front of the mirror, she carefully tucked her hair up under a beige beret until not one blonde strand showed. With her suntanned skin, she was one color all over. Except for her blue eyes. They reflected the apprehension she felt.

She knew nothing could stop Kevin now. He was determined to go around the headland. And in spite of everything, she wanted to go with him. But it was hazardous. There was danger from the tide, if their timing wasn't perfect. There was danger from the witch, if she should be on her rock. The cove was hers, and there were signs posted on this side of the headland. One said: PRIVATE PROPERTY. DO NOT PASS THIS POINT. Another said: TRESPASSERS WILL BE

PROSECUTED. A third warned: BEWARE TREACHEROUS
SEAS. The signs were old and rusted, but they couldn't
claim they hadn't seen them. They would be tres-
passing. Witch or not, the woman could have them
arrested.

And then there was the danger of the cove itself,
with its ghosts walking the beach and wailing in the
cavern. And the frightening memory of Stash, whose
bones were in that urn.

Christie thought of her mother, and almost wished
she were here to stop them from going. It was true,
they weren't breaking their promise to her, but . . .

"Chris!" Kevin called impatiently. "What's holding
you up? It's time to go."

When she came out of her room, he was ready and
waiting in olive drab pants and sweatshirt.

"I've left the lights on in case we're late, and locked
the doors," he said. "Come on."

He stuffed his little transistor radio into a pocket
and they raced down the stairs and across the beach
to the headland. There was no time now to think
fearful thoughts. They were going into the haunted
cove—that was settled. It was only a question of
watching the tide and choosing the right moment.

11

BEWARE TREACHEROUS SEAS

The swells rolling in toward the headland were farther out than Kevin and Christie had ever seen them before, but still they curled up into gentle breakers that sent the water foaming in to splash against the rock. Only when it slid back could they see the sandy shore that curved around the base of the cliff. But that glimpse was enough to tell them they could make their run barefoot, without fear of jagged rocks beneath the foam.

"There won't be time between breakers to get clear around the headland," said Kevin. "One of them will catch us halfway. But if we want to get there before the witch comes out, we'd better go now."

He began to roll up his pant legs, and Christie followed suit.

"Get them as high as you can," he said, "and we'll carry our sneakers."

When their pants were rolled above their knees, they took off their sneakers and waited, watching the succession of breakers. Sometimes they followed swiftly, one upon the other. If they were caught then, they'd be soaked by the splashing. But sometimes there was a lull between them, and the water slid back a long way.

"Now!" Kevin commanded suddenly, and started running.

The sea was beginning its long slide back and Christie darted after her brother, both of them racing to beat the next breaker. Luck was with them, and they were almost around the headland when the gentle foam caught them, swirling only halfway up to their knees.

"Keep running," Kevin shouted, as the water slid back, "and don't stop for anything. Just follow me."

They swung into the witch's cove, and without even slowing for a glance at her rock, headed for the clump of trees above the tide mark. Sprinting at top speed, Kevin lunged beneath the branches, and seconds later Christie dove under, beside him.

"We made it!" Kevin gasped, grinning exuberantly at his sister.

Caught up in the excitement of their adventure, she grinned back, though there was alarm in the pounding of her heart, and she was too out of breath to speak.

They were lying under a low-slung pine on the outer rim of the cluster of trees, and now Kevin began to crawl farther in toward the center. Christie crawled after him until they reached three sturdy trunks that stood together like triplets, with their branches dropping in a gently swaying circle.

It was like being inside the walls of a round green hut, warm and safe in the pine-scented air, with a soft bed of brown needles beneath them. But the lovely feeling was mixed with anxiety, for Christie felt that nothing was safe in this cove. From the center of this snug green shelter, they couldn't see out, but the witch, from her rock, or perhaps even from her house, could have seen them running in.

"Is she out there?" Christie asked.

Kevin crawled to the opposite rim of the circle, facing the rock fortress, and carefully parted the pine branches. For what seemed a long time, he stared out without answering.

"Well, is she?" asked Christie impatiently.

"No—no, we beat her," said Kevin. "But from here I can see something else, something your friend Mora doesn't know."

"What?"

"I can see how her witch gets out to her rock, and she doesn't ride any broomstick."

"How does she get there?" asked Christie, crawling to a spot beside him.

"Look for yourself!"

Christie peered out. At first she saw nothing but the great square rock rising up out of the sea, with its twisted coven tree leaning down over the side. And then, beyond its branches, she saw the bridge. It looked small and fragile, almost like a toy hanging in space, but it was a real suspension bridge, wide enough for one person to cross at a time.

It seemed to be made of heavy rope with boards fastened along its bottom like a wooden sidewalk, and there was nothing to hang onto but a railing of rope on each side. It stretched across the water from the rock toward the land and disappeared behind the tops of the trees in front of the house. She couldn't see the other end, but Kevin had moved to a new viewpoint.

"It isn't anchored to the porch," he said. "It must come out near the top of the cavern."

At the mention of the cavern, Christie scanned the cove for the place where it opened out onto the shore. All along the beach, big logs lay piled one upon the other where the sea rolled them, and here and there, an immense stump stood, up-ended, with its thick roots reaching out like the curving tentacles of an octopus.

Above the driftwood, the beach met the cliff. Somewhere at the bottom of that sloping rock there had to be an opening. Christie searched its craggy surface until she spotted a dark, shadowed place that looked as if it had been gouged out by the sea.

"I think I've found it," she said.

"What?" asked Kevin, moving back to peer out beside her.

"The entrance to the cavern. See that dark hollow above the piles of driftwood? It's just this side of the bridge."

"Yeah, I see it. Looks like a cave," said Kevin. "Only it must be huge inside to have stairs that go all the way up to the house. I bet if we were down there by that driftwood, we could see the urn."

"I don't want to see it," said Christie, with a shiver. "It's bad enough to be this close. I can feel it from here."

"Now you're imagining," said Kevin.

"No, I really feel something. I don't know what it is, but—"

"Maybe it's Stash," said Kevin.

"Maybe," said Christie. "It's like the feeling I had when I saw him. Something—bad. I think we ought to get out of here."

"You mean, go back now, without seeing the witch?"

"I don't think she's coming out," said Christie.

"Of course she is. She comes out every night."

At that moment they were startled by the distant trumpeting of sea lions, and looking out toward the horizon, they saw the dark bodies of the herd barreling inshore.

"She must be coming out now," said Kevin.

They looked up toward the little bridge. It was swaying slightly as if someone might have started across it. Christie held her breath, waiting in suspense for the first glimpse of the black-cloaked figure. If she came, then Mora's spell had failed. But though the bridge kept on swaying, no figure appeared.

"It must be the breeze moving it," said Kevin, at last. "Boy, I'd hate to cross that bridge in a winter gale."

The sea lions had reached the witch's rock now and were churning around it, while one bewhiskered bull popped up and down, barking as if he were calling her. From somewhere on the housetop, the gulls answered in excited shrieks, but they didn't fly down. Apparently they, too, were waiting.

Nervously, Christie kept her eyes on the bridge, while Kevin watched the noisy antics of the mammoth bull and his harem. The sun moved down the sky until it was a rose-red ball resting on the sea, but still the woman had not appeared.

"She isn't coming," said Christie positively.

"Why do you keep saying that?" asked Kevin. "She's just late, that's all."

"It's more than that," said Christie. "She isn't

127

coming because she *can't*. Mora put a spell on her."

"That's ridiculous," Kevin scoffed. "Mora couldn't put a spell on a witch."

"Then why isn't she out on her rock?"

"I don't know," he admitted.

"Look!" said Christie. "The sun is setting, and she's always been here, playing her flute, long before it went down."

"What kind of spell did Mora put on her?" asked Kevin, intrigued.

"I'm not supposed to tell you," said Christie, "but I didn't promise I wouldn't."

"It had something to do with that cigar box, didn't it?"

"I'll make you a bargain," said Christie. "I'll tell you about the box, if you'll tell me what came last night when the witch blew those high notes on her flute."

"It's a deal," said Kevin. "You start first, and maybe by the time you finish, she'll be out there calling with her flute, and I can *show* you."

Christie didn't believe that, but she told him about the clay image—and how Mora had said a spell over it while she nailed it in the box. Then after she'd gone home, she had done it all over again with a stronger spell she'd found in her sister's book.

"That must be the one that worked," said Christie, peering through the pine needles," because she hasn't come out. And I don't think she can—not until Mora decides to let her."

Could it be possible that she was locked inside by Mora's spell? Kevin wondered.

"That's crazy!" he said aloud, still watching hopefully for her to appear.

"Lots of things seem crazy," said Christie, "but that doesn't stop them from happening."

"You're right!" said Kevin excitedly. "Look out there!"

Christie knelt beside him. "I don't see anything."

"Way out," said Kevin. "Coming in from the ocean."

"Dolphins!" said Christie, with a shriek of delight. Beyond the rock fortress and the sea lions, a pod of them was vaulting in toward the cove.

"*That's* what came last night when she blew those high notes," said Kevin. "Do they look like a coven of witches?"

"I don't know," said Christie breathlessly. "They might be magic. Look how they arch through the water—and they're almost pink."

"So's the sea," said Kevin. "It's the reflection of the sunset color in the clouds. But I think they really answered her flute last night. I don't know what brought them in now, unless it was the roaring of the sea lions."

"We'll never know," said Christie, letting her imagination take over. "Maybe she sent out some kind of radar we couldn't hear. They *could* be enchanted Look what they're doing!"

Together, they watched as the dolphins bumped the fat sea lions with their long noses, and then leapt grinning into the air and whirled around to do it all over again, as if the whole thing were a game or a dance.

Suddenly Christie noted with alarm that the last glow was fading out of the sky. "Kevin!" she cried. "We forgot about the tide!"

"Holy smoke!" he said. "Grab your sneakers and

let's get out of here!"

Sneakers in hand, they crawled out from under the branches and raced toward the headland. One look told them they were too late. The surf was already crashing against the cliff, sending up its blinding fountains of foam. And the wind was stronger than they had realized in their shelter of pines. It was driving the breakers in, one behind the other, so that there was no time for the water to slide back and let them pass.

"We have to get through!" said Christie desperately.

"We can't," said Kevin. "We'd drown if we tried."

"But if we watched for the right moment—"

"I wouldn't take a chance. We couldn't fight those breakers. They'd smash us against the cliff and that heavy spray would come down and smother us."

"Oh, Kevin," Christie groaned, "what'll we do?"

"Get out some other way," he said, trying to sound more confident than he felt.

"There isn't any other way, except the cavern. Mora told us that."

"Well, you spotted the entrance. Maybe we could make it up those stairs after dark."

"If you think I'd go in there, with Stash's bones in that urn!"

"Would you rather spend the night in this cove?"

"With all those ghosts walking the beach and wailing?" Christie shuddered at the thought.

"We don't have much choice," said Kevin. "We're trapped."

12 DANGEROUS CROSSING

There was nothing to do but run back to the trio of pines, for if the witch should happen to be looking out of the right window, she might spot them. Kevin lingered outside the sheltering branches to study the contour of the land as it sloped up steeply from the shore to the old house and stable. Then he crawled inside.

With the sun gone the wind was cold, and Christie was rolling down her pant legs. While Kevin rolled down his own, he pondered their problem.

"I suppose we could hide here until the next low tide," he said.

"When would that be?" asked Christie, slipping her feet into her sneakers.

"Probably twelve or thirteen hours from now."

"But that's no good. We'd still be here all night."

"And in the morning, the tide won't even be a minus."

Kevin saw the distress deepen in his sister's face.

"Then what can we do?" she asked.

"There's a chance we could scale the slope behind us," he said, tieing his shoe laces. "There's a good screen of trees to shield us from the house, but it's awfully steep. And it'll be dark before we know it."

"Then let's go," said Christie decisively.

Outside the circle of pines, they stood looking up at the slope. The climb would be rough and slippery, and in places the trees grew so close together that they couldn't see what lay beyond them.

"Chris," Kevin warned earnestly, "I'm not sure you can make it. You could have a bad fall. I may not even be able to make it myself."

But Christie was not to be deterred. "We can try," she said. "I'd rather try anything than stay in this cove tonight."

There was no trail, but they started with Kevin in the lead. He chose a winding route that took them up gradually, twisting back and forth between young trees and bushes that gave them something to hang onto.

Following close on his heels, Christie grasped each trunk and branch as he let go, pulling herself slowly upward from one anchorage to another. But even though he was trying to make the climb as safe as possible, the going was rough. The slope became steeper, the reaching and pulling harder.

They clung close to the earth, seeing no farther ahead than the next hand-hold. And then suddenly, beyond a stand of fir, the slope ended and they were faced with a vertical wall of rock. It rose some twelve feet or more above them, and there was no way around it. They had to go up—or back.

"We'd better go back," said Kevin.

"No," Christie protested. "There are little holes we can get our toes into, and ledges we can grab hold of."

It was true, there were little round hollows here and there in the rock, and narrow outcroppings that might serve as handholds, but they were shallow and treacherous.

"If we slipped, or the ledge we grabbed onto came loose, it'd be a long fall," said Kevin. "It's too dangerous."

"Please," Christie pleaded, "let's try it—just a little way up. If we can't make it, I'll go back. But I have a feeling the cove is more dangerous than this cliff."

"Okay, then," Kevin agreed, "but only a little way. I'll boost you up, and you see what you can get hold of."

The round hollows near the bottom barely gave her a toe-hold, but with Kevin to support her, Christie began to pull herself up the wall. The sharp edges of rock tore at her fingers, but the menace she felt in the cove was greater than her pain, and she grasped at one outcropping above another until she was standing on her brother's shoulders.

"How is it now?" asked Kevin, keeping a tight hold on her ankles.

"The top is still about three feet beyond my reach," she told him.

"Is there anything solid you could hold onto, if you got up there?"

"There's a bare root of a tree hanging down over the edge—a big root."

"Then I'll try to get you up to it," said Kevin. "Lean hard against the cliff—let it carry as much of your weight as you can."

"Okay."

"And whatever you've got hold of, hang on tight, because I'll have to let go of your ankles."

"I will," said Christie, not daring to look down.

With his sister balanced precariously on his shoulders, Kevin began to move up, testing each crack and outcropping to make sure it could bear their double weight. Slowly, daring no more than a few inches at a time, he edged up, clinging grimly to the stone until it cut into his palms. When he was some two feet above the ground, he paused.

"Can you reach it now?" he asked.

Letting go of the little ledge that had been her anchorage, Christie clawed her way up to the root.

"I've got hold of it!" she said.

"Can you pull yourself up?"

"I'll try."

She felt sick and dizzy, and her arms were strained, her muscles quivering from the climb. She waited a moment, leaning against the rock to summon her courage. Then with her feet scrabbling for a toe-hold, she pulled herself hand over hand up the length of the root until she could swing over the edge of the cliff and onto solid ground. Unable to speak, she lay gasping and sobbing with relief, while the pounding of her heart shook her body.

Far below her, Kevin called: "Are you all right?"

"I'm up! I'm safe!" she answered, still gasping.

"I'm coming," said Kevin.

With no one to support him, his climb was even more hazardous, and he moved up cautiously, knowing that if just one toe or handhold gave way under him, he could crash to the bottom of the cliff. But at length he pulled himself over the edge and collapsed beside Christie.

"Wow!" he breathed. "Let's not do that again!"

"Let's not!" she said.

While they rested briefly, Kevin took out his radio

and pulled up the aerial. With the volume down low, he turned from station to station, but there was no news of the bank robbers. They seemed to have disappeared. He put the radio back in his pocket. The light was fading fast, and another long, steep slope stretched ahead of them. He and Christie struggled up it, protected by a thick stand of trees.

"We must be a good hundred feet above the beach," Kevin said as he paused to get his breath.

Wearily, they pushed through a tangle of branches only to be confronted by another cliff.

Christie stared at it, close to tears, "I can't," she said despairingly.

"We can't go back," said Kevin. "Not down that cliff."

"I can't go up, either," said Christie. "My legs are shaking so I can hardly stand."

Kevin stood surveying the barrier in front of them. "This one's not too bad," he said. "There's a spot where it's not more than seven feet high. I could get you up it, but I think I'd better go first and find out what's ahead."

"You won't be gone long!" said Christie, alarmed at the thought of being alone in the darkening woods.

"Only long enough to see if we can make it," Kevin promised. "You rest till I get back. If there are no more cliffs, and the gate's open, I can get you up this one easily."

Christie supported her brother as he scrambled up the wall of eroded earth. When he had pulled himself over the top, he whispered down to her, "Stay right here, so I can find you." Then he disappeared into the higher level of woods.

Christie sank down at the base of the cliff. Her

body was trembling from the long, hard pull, and it was good to stop forcing herself to go on. She sat quietly, leaning back against the hard earth while her breathing eased and her pulse slowed.

Climbing up the long ascent from the beach, there had been only one thought in her mind: to reach the top. Now she became aware of other things: the increasing darkness—the stillness. There was no barking to echo through the cove, no screaming of birds. The sea lions must have gone back to their rookery, the gulls to their roost.

And the dolphins, so pink and graceful, vaulting over the tinted sea—where had they come from, and why? Could they have been answering a call from the witch?

She thought of Mora and the second spell she had put on the clay image in the box. It had worked. The witch had not come out. She wondered what kind of spell it had been.

For some reason she couldn't explain, even to herself, she didn't want the witch harmed. Perhaps it was because of the music she had played on her flute last night—so truly magic.

She thought suddenly of the young couple that had been turned to stone. In the rush to get around the headland to the shelter beneath the trees, she and Kevin hadn't seen them. And when they had raced back, only to find the tide too high, they had been too upset to notice. But they *must* have been there!

The whole terrible history of the cove flooded back into her mind, and with it the uneasy feeling she had had when she'd knelt in their pine shelter, watching for the witch.

The trees around her now were no longer green but black. She realized it was night, and Kevin had not come back. She was alone somewhere near the haunted house and the witch, and the wind was sighing through the forest.

She sat perfectly still, trying to see in the darkness, and then she heard a sound that stopped her heart. It was faint, yet near—a mournful murmuring sound—and suddenly her pulse was throbbing in her throat and ears so that she could hardly hear it. After a moment it came again, louder this time, like a deep sobbing that rose to a thin wail and then faded in a moan that slid down the scale like music.

Theodora's organ! That's what she was hearing. And the hands touching its keys could not be human. Just as Mora had said, it was eerie and unreal, but it *was* the sound of an organ. There was a silence, and then it began again—a pleading lament that shifted from one key to another, as though the ghost of Theodora were trying to find the melody she had once played in such desperation: "Nearer My God To Thee."

Christie was sitting, rigid, listening to the ghostly music, when she heard the whisper of her name. For one awful instant she thought Theodora was calling her. Then the whisper came again, sharp and insistent.

"Chris! Are you there?"

"Yes," she answered softly, knowing it was her brother.

He swung over the edge of the cliff and dropped down beside her.

"Kevin," she whispered, "I've just heard it."

"Heard what?"

"The ghost of Theodora playing her organ. Listen!"

"I haven't time," he said. "I've got a lot to tell you."

There was a hushed urgency in his voice that warned her it was important.

"First of all, the gate's padlocked. That means we can't get out—not until morning, and then only if the tide's low enough."

"Oh, no!" said Christie, appalled. "We can't go down that cliff. You said so yourself. Down would be worse than up. We'd fall and be killed."

"No, we can't go down that way."

"Then you mean the—?"

"Never mind *how*," Kevin cut in. "We're not going anywhere, this minute."

The melancholy strain moaned through the organ pipes again.

"Hear it?" Christie whispered.

"Yeah," said Kevin, pausing to listen in amazement. "It does sound like a ghost." But after a moment he dismissed it with his usual practicality. "Must be the wind stirring the organ."

"How could it be the wind?"

"I don't know. Maybe there's a draft from some of those old gables or turrets that's sucking down into the pipes," he said impatiently. "It doesn't matter, anyway. I've got more important things to talk about."

His nervous insistence made Christie uneasy. "Tell me," she said.

"Well, there weren't any more cliffs and I made it

139

up to the stable. Then I sneaked around the back to where I could see the driveway. The gate wasn't open the way it was yesterday. It was closed and locked. And that isn't all."

"What else?"

"Chris, remember the camper we saw in the fog?"

"Yes."

"It was in the garage. I could see it through a crack where the old wall had split."

"But when we saw the camper there was a man in it—"

"There sure was. And there was another man out on the point behind the tombstone—a *man*, Chris, not the ghost of Stash."

"Why do you say it was a man?"

"Because I saw him at the upstairs window of the house."

"You did?"

"They didn't have those back blinds down, but the curtains were drawn. It was almost dark, but not quite, and he pulled back the curtain just enough to look out. I saw his face, Chris. He was lean and dark and he had a beard."

"That could be Stash—his ghost, I mean."

"It could be somebody else. Do you know what I think?"

"No."

"I think the bank robbers are in that house with the witch. That's why she didn't come out. And that's why she keeps to herself. She's one of their gang and this is their hideout."

"Oh, Kevin, that's crazy," said Christie. "I don't believe it."

"Not any crazier than her being a witch."

He took the transistor out of his pocket, and Christie heard him snap on the switch.

"Shut it off," she whispered in alarm. "If they should hear it—"

"They won't," he said, keeping the volume so low he had to hold the tiny speaker against his ear to hear it himself.

While he listened, Christie thought back to the moment when she had seen the face of the man behind the tombstone. If he was a robber, no wonder there had been such menace in his eyes. But several questions disturbed her.

"Kevin," she asked, "what do you think that man was doing out on the point?"

"Casing the place, I suppose."

"But if this is their regular hideout, why should he have to case it?"

Kevin was silent a moment. "You could be right," he said thoughtfully.

"And when I saw him, why didn't he grab me, or both of us? I had a feeling all the time he was behind us, following us."

"For one thing, he didn't grab us because he couldn't get over that fence. He must have found some way to get through, way out on the point, and he'd have had to go back the same way, so we'd have been pretty far ahead. And for another," said Kevin, "you thought he was a ghost named Stash— and *he* heard you say it."

"That's right," Christie admitted. "But there's something else. They didn't move in on the witch then, because she was on her rock last night *after*

141

we saw them, remember? That's when we heard her beautiful music, and you saw her call in the dolphins."

"Yeah," said Kevin. "So maybe we scared them off—temporarily. Maybe they figured they'd better get out of there in case we reported seeing them and somebody called the police."

"But we only told Mommy about the ghost, not the man in the camper."

"I bet it was that ghost stuff that made them figure they were safe. They probably cased the joint again, in the night, and then moved in on her."

"Kevin—that means she's their hostage."

"Could be," he said, "and if they catch us, they'll have two more."

"Hostages sometimes get—murdered," said Christie, her throat closing on the word.

"Yeah." He shut off the radio. "There's nothing on the news," he said, putting it away. "Chris, we've got to get down from here before daylight."

"How?"

"The cavern. There's no other way."

He could barely see her face in the dim light filtering down from the stars, but he knew how she felt.

"There's nothing to be afraid of," he said. "You didn't really see a ghost out there, you know. You saw a man. And he's the one we've got to get away from—him and his partner. They're the ones who might kill us, not the ghosts."

"But how can we even find the entrance to the cavern in the dark?"

"That's going to be the tricky part," said Kevin. "I think we're just about on a level with it now. But we'll have to push through the woods until we get to the house."

"The house! But they'll be standing watch like that man you saw—one upstairs and one down."

"I know it. We can't afford to make a sound. If we as much as stumble on a stone—"

"We're sure to stumble if we can't see."

"That's why we have to go now, Chris. There's a new moon tonight. I saw it when I was up by the stable. It'll be low and going down fast, but it'll give us just a little light—all we'll get before daybreak."

"But if we can see, then they can see *us*."

"We'll be working our way down under the front porch," said Kevin. "I don't think they'll be looking there. They'll be watching the driveway and the street."

"I'm scared," said Christie, with a tremor in her voice.

"So am I. We'd be crazy not to be," said Kevin. "But we've got just one tough stretch: from the edge of the trees to the entrance to the cavern. Once we're inside that, we'll be in the dark."

"With the urn," said Christie.

"Don't think about that. Right now, just think about getting through the trees. Come on. Give me your hand."

Christie put her hand in his and they moved very slowly through the dark firs, trying to step lightly so that no twig would break with a sharp sound beneath their feet. The black columns seemed endless, and Kevin and Christie walked with their free hands extended in front of them, so as to escape collision with a tree trunk.

Finally the firs thinned out, and rising before them was the huge black bulk of the house, with a pale slit of light showing around the edges of the window blinds. They stood staring at it until they could see the big porch outlined dimly against the night sky. It was above them, and somewhere under it must be the entrance to the cavern. But before they could reach it, they would have to step out from under the shelter of the trees and onto an open slope. The light from the little crescent moon was faint, revealing only that the land under their feet would be rough and rocky.

"Take just one step at a time," Kevin whispered, "and don't put your weight down until you've tested to make sure what you're stepping on is solid. I'll go first."

But he waited, gripping his sister's hand hard.

"They ought to have a sign here that says DANGEROUS CROSSING," she whispered shakily.

13

NIGHT IN THE COVE

They stood a moment longer, staring across the open space that stretched ahead of them. It couldn't be more than thirty feet, yet it seemed like three hundred. Every inch of it held a double threat, for there was not only the danger underfoot, but the menace of unseen eyes above them.

Big windows overlooked the porch, and there were no slits of light showing around them. A man with a gun could be sitting there in the dark guarding the approach to the front of the house.

"We're going to make it!" Kevin whispered. Then he moved boldly out of the shadows onto the open slope. Testing each step, he walked silent as a cat in his sneakers.

Christie tried to see the places where he had found secure footing, but the infant moon was already lying on its back so low over the horizon that she could barely make out the ground beneath her own feet.

They longed to run to the comparative safety beneath the porch, but they forced themselves to walk, step by cautious step, not even daring to lift their eyes to look toward their goal.

When she could no longer see the ground, Christie thought the little moon had set, but Kevin whispered softly, "We made it, Chris. We're under the porch."

Half of the threat was over. Their crossing hadn't been seen.

"There've got to be stairs," Kevin whispered, "but I can't see them from here."

"Josef saw Theodora go down from the porch, the night she drowned," Christie reminded him.

"Then they must be at the far end, and they probably lead right to the cavern and the bridge."

"It's an awfully long porch," said Christie, with dread.

"And the ground under here is more stony. So take it easy, Chris. They can't see us now, but they could sure hear us if we sent a rock rattling down over the roof of the cavern."

The walk under the porch was as harrowing as the first stretch had been, for it was darker now, with even greater danger of betraying themselves by a misstep. But at last Kevin turned back to whisper, "I can see the stairs, Chris. They're just a couple of yards ahead, and they slope down into a dark hollow that must be the cavern."

Perhaps it was Christie's terror of the cavern that distracted her, but with her next step she stumbled, and a rock slid out from under her feet. She stood frozen with horror as it rolled down the slope, the noise of it growing louder with each bounce.

"Run!" Kevin whispered frantically.

Confused, she turned back in panic toward the woods.

"No, Chris, no! *This way!*" he whispered in desperation.

But she didn't hear him. Running wildly in the

wrong direction, she was sending more stones spinning out onto the slope where they rattled down
over the rock roof of the cavern like a small landslide.

Kevin tore after her, ignoring the stones his own
feet were dislodging to add to the clamor. Just as he
caught up with her, Theodora's pipe organ thundered
out the old hymn "Nearer My God to Thee" until the
timbers above them creaked with the vibration. They
stood stunned for a moment; then Kevin grabbed
his sister's arm.

"You crazy?" he cried, his voice covered by the
booming music. "You're running the wrong way. Our
only chance is the cavern!"

He pulled her after him, and the stones continued
to fly out from under their feet as they ran back
toward the stairs. The organ stopped as abruptly as
it had begun.

"Dive into the cavern!" Kevin commanded in a
whisper.

Instinctively, Christie shrank back from the
yawning blackness, but he clung to her arm, dragging her in with him.

"We've got to get down fast," he said, reaching
out in the darkness to find the stair rail. "If she
hadn't slowed them up with that organ, they'd be
on us already."

He found the railing and guided Christie's hand to
it. "Hold on tight," he said, "and take one step at a
time, but for gosh sake don't hang back!"

With the sky blotted out by the ceiling of the
cavern, they moved down in total darkness. Christie
wondered when they would reach the burial urn. It

148

was useless to look at their feet, for they were lost in blackness, and she raised her eyes, half expecting to see the white wraith of Stash's ghost appear before them. Instead, she was blinded by a dazzle of light filling the cavern.

"Holy smoke! Floodlights!" Kevin whispered.

He glanced up toward the entrance. No one had yet appeared, and fortunately he and Christie had come far enough down the curving stairs to be out of sight of anyone standing on the porch.

"Maybe we've still got a chance," he whispered. "Run for your life!" And leading his sister, he bounded down, two steps at a time.

There must have been more than two hundred of them winding down under the high arched ceiling of rock, but Kevin and Christie were barely aware of the immensity of the cavern. Nor could they pause beside the burial urn as they raced toward the bottom, the soft thud of their sneakers drowned out by the sound of the sea.

The lower entrance was wide, like a huge mouth, and it was easy to see how a great wave could have rushed in and overtaken Stash. But now, looking out, Kevin saw that other floodlights lit the beach.

He glanced back up the stairs. Still no one was following them. Whoever was watching expected to spot them as they came out of the cave.

"We've got to crawl on our bellies into the drift-wood," he told Christie, leading her to the narrow corner of the cavern's mouth.

They dropped flat and snaked their way out onto the beach. With their clothes the color of sand and wood and sea grasses, it would be hard to pick them out. Keeping their heads low, they edged into a hollow between two logs. From the house far above them, they could now pass for part of the heaped-up driftwood.

Kevin longed to know what was going on up there, but he couldn't risk raising his head above the log. "Chris," he whispered, "I'm going to work my way down to that big stump. From there, maybe I can see something."

"I'll follow you," she said.

"If you do, don't raise your head," he warned, "not even if the lights go out. It might be a trick to catch us."

He began to work his way down the beach toward the huge upended stump, slithering between logs, and at times sliding very slowly up and over them into the next hollow. When he reached the stump, he pulled himself up inside its curling roots. The great bulk of it shielded him from the lights, and he peered up toward the house.

It was hard to see beyond the glare, but the porch was empty, the heavy drapes still drawn over the big windows. Evidently the men had no intention of betraying their presence. The rest of the house was in shadow, but he knew that any one of the small windows could be open, and a man behind the curtain could be looking straight down the sights of a rifle to where he stood.

The lights went off and everything was black. He tried to see Christie, but his eyes were still blinded from the glare. The darkness lengthened out, and he began to think they might have had time to run down the beach toward the little shelter of trees.

Then the floods blazed on again. Just as he had sus-

pected, it had been a trick. If they'd been running, they'd have been caught in the stream of light.

He looked for his sister, but he couldn't find her.

"I'm here," she said, from below his feet. "I crawled the way you did. I didn't raise my head." She pulled herself up beside him in the shadow of the stump.

Kevin peered up toward the house. Nothing seemed to have changed there. He glanced at the driftwood around them. The stump was in the midst of it, with logs piled up behind it all the way to the cliff. On the ocean side, more logs lay between them and the smooth beach. He counted them. There were six.

"Chris," he said, "take a look at those six logs. Memorize how they lie and figure out the best way to get across them in the dark."

While she studied them, he glanced toward the mouth of the cavern and the house. There was no change—no one in sight.

"If the lights go out again," he said, "we're going to get across those logs as fast as we can and run like mad down the beach toward our place under the trees."

He had no sooner said the words than the lights went out. In the darkness, they scrambled across the logs until they reached the sand.

"Now run!" Kevin commanded. "And if the lights come on, flop—and don't move."

Their eyes were becoming adjusted to the darkness, and the starlight guided them as they raced along the smooth beach. No floods came on, and as they approached the headland, they turned up toward the little trio of pines they had left at dusk.

When they'd crawled back under the branches, they collapsed, panting, on the soft blanket of needles. For a long time they lay still while the hammering of their hearts eased and their breathing got back to normal.

"It's like coming home," Christie sighed at last. "I wish we'd never left this place. It's my fault. And now those men know we're here."

"And we know *they're* here," said Kevin.

"If only I hadn't stumbled! D'you think they might decide all those falling rocks were just a landslide?

I mean, one that happened without anybody being there to set it off?"

"I doubt it," said Kevin, "but that woman sure did her best to cover for us. She must have gone for that keyboard the minute she heard the first rock. She was booming out all the time we were running back and forth." He chuckled. "Between the threat of somebody sneaking up on them and the thunder she was making, those robbers must have been in a state of total confusion. That's why we had time to get down inside the cavern before they got the flood-lights on."

"I wonder why she played 'Nearer My God To Thee'?"

"I think it was a sort of signal—like a cry for help. She probably figures everyone around here knows the story of Theodora, and that was her way of saying she was in trouble."

"She's in terrible trouble, isn't she?"

"She sure is, and that ought to prove to you she has no magic powers. If she did have, she'd have gotten herself out of it."

"I don't know," said Christie thoughtfully. "Maybe it just proves Mora's spell is more powerful. She might have been saying that one out of her sister's book just about the time those robbers came back."

"Chris," said Kevin impatiently, "Mora has nothing to do with this."

"She could have," Christie insisted. "She cured my arm."

"You don't honestly believe that, do you?"

"Why not? The numbness went away."

"I told you it would. The 'cure' had nothing to do

153

with witchcraft. That idea was all in your mind. When Mora burned that incense and said some crazy words—"

"Incense? How did you know?"

"I was there," said Kevin. "I didn't want to tell you, but I saw you drink the potion."

"You did?" Christie was stunned.

"I've been wanting to ask you: How did it taste?"

"Good, I guess," said Christie, trying to remember back.

"Like what?"

"Well, sort of like coconut milk and—maybe ginger—and some kinds of spices."

"I thought so," said Kevin. "She didn't get that recipe out of any magic book. Her mother is a gourmet cook. Mora just made the potion out of things her mother happened to have in her kitchen."

"Maybe so," said Christie, "but I don't think that proves much." There were a lot of things that couldn't be explained so easily, she thought, including the green eye. But she didn't mention that to Kevin.

He had already dismissed the whole subject and was crawling out through the branches to look up the beach. A moment later, he was back.

"It's all dark out there," he said. "I think they're lying low, waiting for daybreak."

"Do you think they'll hurt her?" asked Christie anxiously.

"By now you can bet they've got her tied up so she can't get near that organ again," said Kevin. "But she's worth more to them alive than dead. If the police catch up with them, she's their ticket out of the trap."

"When's low tide?" asked Christie.

"Too many hours after daybreak. That's what worries me."

"D'you think they'll come down here looking for us?"

"I don't know," Kevin said. "I think they'll figure they're safer holed up where they are. But if they should see us go around the headland, they might get out of there pronto, and take her with them. What I've got to figure out is a way to save her."

Suddenly he remembered his radio. He took it out and pulled up the aerial. At length he tuned into a newscast and listened with his ear against the speaker.

"They're the bank robbers, all right!" he burst out. "They stole that camper. The police found the owner tied up in his cabin back in the mountains. But now their trail is cold. We're the only ones who know where they're hiding out."

"Golly!" Christie breathed apprehensively. "What are we going to do?"

"Pray for another fog, like that one yesterday— a real pea-souper," said Kevin, shutting off the radio. "They wouldn't risk starting out in that, and we could get around the headland without their seeing us."

"But *could* we get around?" asked Christie. "If the tide isn't minus, and we couldn't see?"

"We won't know the answer to that till morning," said Kevin. "For now, we'd better try to sleep."

They lay on their backs, staring up at the dark branches. A few hours earlier, Christie had been horrified at the thought of spending the night in this cove; now it was doubly menacing. But she was more tired than she'd ever been in her life—too tired to think, too tired even to be afraid. Between the pine needles above her, she spotted a single star, and focusing her eyes upon it, she drifted off to sleep.

Kevin was tired, too, but his mind was wide awake and he lay thinking of the two robbers up in the old house, and the helpless woman. Even if he and Christie could get around the headland and notify the police, that wouldn't guarantee her safety. They could use her as a hostage to force their way out, and once they got away, she'd be expendable.

He thought about the way the house was built, with that solid wall across the back and only two small windows. And the cliffs all around. In such a house, two men could hold off the police a long time, and if finally they had to surrender. . . . Either way, the woman could die.

He remembered how she'd stood on her rock last night, with the gulls and sea lions around her, and how the dolphins had answered her flute. Christie was right about one thing: There was something special about the music that came out of her flute.

Suddenly a plan came into his mind, a plan that might save her. It was a daring idea. It would be dangerous. He'd be risking his own life. But it might work.

He got up and crawled out from under the pines. The tide was coming in, rolling far up toward their shelter. The wind was still fresh, and though he could hardly believe his ears, he heard a wailing. He listened intently. For a moment there was only the sound of the breakers, and then the wailing rose above them, a long drawn out cry that was like the blending of many voices. The wailing of the ghosts!

His heart thumped against his chest, and he stared down the beach, but he couldn't see any filmy white figures walking there. A little gust of wind sent the loose sand spinning up into his face, and the wailing grew louder. The wind! That was it, he told himself. The wail had to be the wind whining up through the long curving cavern.

He looked up toward the old house set into its hill and barely visible beneath the starlit sky.

"I'm going to do it!" he whispered to himself.

Then he crawled back under the pines, and curling up behind his sister to keep her warm, he fell asleep.

14

KEVIN'S PLAN

Kevin woke out of a deep sleep, surprised, for an instant, to see a green ceiling of pine branches above him. Then he remembered everything, including his plan.

Christie was still asleep on the soft bed of needles. He wondered what time it was. It could be as early as daybreak, for the light filtering down through the trees was a pale gray. There was none of the brightness of sunshine, nor was there any wind, for the branches drooped motionless around them.

He peered out and saw the pea-soup fog he'd wanted, so thick it completely blotted out the ocean. He crawled out and ran down to the water's edge. The tide was low and the sea calm. Only one small breaker foamed up onto the shore.

The cove, the house, the witch's rock—all were lost in the white smother of mist. He couldn't see more than twenty feet in any direction, nor could anyone see him. It was perfect for his plan.

He ran back to wake Christie, and while she came to slowly, he turned on his radio to check the time. To his amazement, it was after ten o'clock.

"Jeepers! We almost slept through low tide," he said. "We've got to go right now, Chris, or we'll miss our chance." He began to pull off his sweatshirt.

"What're you doing?" she asked in puzzlement.

"Getting out of my clothes," he said, "and you'd better start doing the same. We can't walk around the headland this morning. The tide's not going to be that low. But the sea's quiet, and we can swim around. Only we can't afford to be weighed down by heavy, water-logged clothes. We'll swim in our T-shirts and shorts."

He began to untie his shoelaces, and automatically Christie pulled her sweater over her head.

"You mean we're going to leave our sweaters and jeans here?" she asked.

"And our sneakers," he said. "We can come back and get them after the police capture those crooks."

He didn't intend to tell her about his plan until they got around the headland to their own cove. For one thing, she still wasn't fully awake. The cold swim would take care of that. For another, she'd be against it and want to argue. But once he'd gotten her safely around, he'd tell her what *she* was to do, and then he'd start back. There'd be no time to argue. He'd have to swim back before the tide got any higher.

He slipped his radio inside one of his sneakers, and then they folded their jeans and sweaters into neat rolls and left them beside the three tree trunks. The fog felt damp and cold on their skin as they ran toward the misty shape of the headland.

"Did you wake up in the night?" Christie asked.

"No, did you?"

"No. I wish I had," she said regretfully. "I suppose I'd have been scared if I'd seen any ghosts—but

I really *wanted* to see them."

Kevin thought of telling her about the wailing, but decided against it. He'd tell her later, when there was more time. They were coming close to the headland now, and he noticed two tall rocks looming up out of the mist, just beyond the swirl of foam.

"Chris, look!" he said, pointing. "Do you know what those rocks are?"

"No."

"They're your young couple."

Christie peered at them in unbelief. From this angle, close at hand, they didn't look like people at all.

"Do you still think your witch turned them to stone with the arrows out of her flute?"

"No," Christie admitted. "I guess not. And I'm awfully glad. They must have gotten out of the cove some other way."

"Probably straight up her stairs," said Kevin.

He strode out into the water, gasping at the cold shock of it. When he was waist deep, he stopped to study the tide as it surged in gently, cresting when it met the cliff.

"We're in luck," he called back. "It's really smooth. There's just one breaker, and we can swim clear out around it."

Christie walked in, gasping, until she stood beside him. "I think the fog's lifting a little," she said.

"Yeah," said Kevin. "We're getting out just in time." And, he thought, I've got to get *back* in time.

"I'll swing out in an arc," he said, "and you swim along with me, on the inside. Ready?"

She nodded and he took off, reaching out in an easy overhand crawl, giving her time to get his pace.

They stroked together, relaxing in the lift and fall of the swells, but keeping their distance from the headland. Halfway around it they rested briefly, treading water, and then swam again. The sight of their own cove in the distance gave them new power, and they pulled toward it eagerly until they could touch bottom and run ashore.

"Oh, Kevin, we're home, we're safe!" cried Christie gratefully, dropping onto the sand.

"But the woman back in that cove isn't," Kevin reminded her.

"We'll call the police right away," she said, starting up.

"No, wait!" said Kevin. "That isn't enough. I did a lot of thinking last night and I figured out a plan. I don't want you to argue with me, Chris, because there isn't time. Just promise you'll do what I tell you."

"What is it?"

"Never mind—just promise. It could save her life —and mine."

"Yours!" Christie cried in amazement.

"And don't question me, either," Kevin commanded. "Take these keys." He took the house keys out of the pocket of his shorts. "And go up and call Terence O'Flaherty. He'll know a lot better than you how to call the police. Tell him everything as fast as you can."

"I will," said Christie, "and then I'll go over to Mora's and make her take that clay image out of the box."

"Okay, but get this, Chris—it's the most important of all."

"What is it?"

161

"I want somebody up on the headland in the place where we've been every night."

"What for?"

"To give me a signal."

"Give *you*—?"

"Listen!" Kevin cut in urgently. "When the police have surrounded the place and are ready to go in after those men, I want somebody to wave a red flag right from that spot where you stood when you saw the two rocks. Remember—out on the point, just out of sight of the house."

"Kevin," Christie demanded sharply, "where will you be?"

"In her cove, where I can see it."

"Are you crazy?" Christie protested. "You can't go back there!"

"I'm going back, Chris. It's the only way to help her. When they give me that signal, I'll go into action. Those robbers will be so busy watching me, the police can come right in behind them."

"But Kevin—"

He had already plunged back into the sea. "Hurry, Chris!" he shouted. "Do what I've told you, and don't forget the signal!"

He began to swim strongly to beat the danger of rising tide and lifting fog.

"Kevin!" Christie screamed desperately.

He paused to wave back at her, then went on, putting all his strength into his strokes.

She watched him an instant in stunned helplessness; then, keys in hand, she streaked up toward the cottage.

Kevin rounded the headland, and with his long, steady crawl, pulled in to shore. The cove was still shrouded in fog. He ran to the pine shelter and quickly changed from wet clothes to dry. After the cold of the water, his pants and sweatshirt felt warm and comforting. He put his transistor into his pocket, and then slipped on his sneakers. When he had tied the laces, he crawled out from under the branches and started up the beach.

The swim twice around the headland had taken a lot of energy and he didn't feel like running, but he ran anyway. It was very important that he reach the cavern while the fog was still heavy enough to cover him. There was a hollow feeling in his stomach and his throat was dry, and suddenly he realized that his symptoms weren't just nervousness. He was thirsty and ravenously hungry. Dinner had been a long time ago. But there was nothing he could do about that now, except to hope that the police would come soon.

He pushed on, passing the logs and the stump that had shielded them from the glare of the floodlights, last night. The floods wouldn't do the robbers any good now. High on its slope, the old house was completly concealed by the mist. A stranger on the beach wouldn't suspect it was there.

Which meant he was equally secure, Kevin thought. Unless one of the men might have come down, under the cover of the fog, to search for last night's trespassers.

The idea gave him a jolt, and he spurted past the entrance to the cavern and flung himself down into a crevice between the heaped-up piles of driftwood. He hadn't seen anyone on the beach, but that didn't mean that someone hadn't seen him.

From his hiding place, Kevin raised his head just

enough to scan the stretch of cove beyond him, to the north. Visibility was poor and if there was a figure moving through the mist in pursuit of him, he couldn't see it.

He looked back to the south, toward the pine shelter from which he had just come, and got a second jolt: From this distance, the headland was obliterated.

The fog that had served him so well until now would defeat him if it lingered. If he couldn't see the headland, then he couldn't see the signal, and without that, he'd be lost. His whole plan depended on timing. He *had* to know when to make his move.

He turned his radio on low and found a newscast. There was nothing more on the robbers, but the time was eleven-fifteen. Just about an hour since he and Christie had started around the promontory.

In that hour he'd gone around it and back, changed his clothes and run the length of the beach to the cavern. Certainly in that time Christie should have reached Mr. O'Flaherty and he should have passed on the word. By now the police should know the story.

But in this little town there might be just one patrol car. They'd need reinforcements. There was no way of knowing how long it would take them to get here. He had to see that red flag and he couldn't —not in this pea soup.

He lay staring up toward the place where the flag should appear, while he tried to think of a way out of his dilemma. It wasn't likely the police would wait till the fog lifted to give him a signal. They'd want to move in fast, he thought, and when they did, the robbers would use the woman as their hostage. Whether the police let them go and take her with them, or whether it all ended in a shoot-out, either way, she'd have about one chance in a thousand.

The headland began to emerge dimly from the mist, and in his excitement he raised himself from between the logs, searching for even a blur of color on its point. It was then his eyes were diverted by something on the beach, and he was appalled to see a man moving toward him with a club in hand. So one of them *had* come down in search of him!

There wasn't any more time for waiting. If he didn't make his move now, his odds would be the same as hers. He darted into the mouth of the cavern, and when he looked back, the man was running toward him.

He sprinted up the stairs. Taking two at a time cut them down to something like one hundred. As he reached the top, he looked down into the cavern's entrance. The man was just coming in.

With a final spurt, Kevin was out at the top. He was very close to the house now. Anyone inside the windows overlooking the porch could see him quite plainly through the mist. He hoped the red flag was out on the point and the police ready to move in, but he couldn't wait to find out. The bulky figure at the foot of the stairs was moving up.

"Hey! Anybody home?" he yelled at the top of his lungs, hoping there were officers within earshot.

There was no answer.

"Hey, is anybody home?" he yelled again.

Out of the corner of his eye, he could see the man in the cavern approaching the top.

Last night as they had crept along under the porch, Kevin had glimpsed the land anchorage of the suspension bridge near the foot of the porch stairs. The bridge was part of his plan, and now he ran out onto it, grasping the rope railing as it swayed under him. He looked back toward the cavern. He couldn't see the man, but he was still inside somewhere in the shadows.

"Hey!" he shouted again toward the house. "If there's anybody in there, I wish you'd come out. I'd like permission to walk on your bridge!"

He backed out a few steps more, clinging to both railings while the bridge continued to sway. The man in hiding stayed where he was, but something was happening inside the house. One drape was opened slightly, then a glass door, and the woman stepped out onto the porch.

Kevin had never seen her without her black cape. She looked much slimmer and she was wearing a dress the color of emeralds. It reminded him of the green eye. He couldn't see the color of her eyes through the mist, but one thing was certain: she had only two. There was no third eye in the middle of her forehead.

"Wait, young man!" she called out to him. "You must not go out on the bridge." Her voice was strong and warm and she spoke with a slight accent.

"Why not?" he called back.

"It is dangerous," she said.

"I'm not afraid," said Kevin, and he turned and ran a few steps out toward her rock. The bridge swayed wildly and he had to stop and hang on.

166

"Please! You must not run!" she called out urgently.

"Okay, I won't run. I'll walk."

She was standing just outside the door, and Kevin heard the low growl of a man's voice from behind the drapes, giving her orders.

He was holding the attention of the gunman, Kevin thought, but the woman was still much too close to him. If the police were ready to move in—and he prayed they were—the man could still seize her and draw her back inside.

"Don't you go out on it?" Kevin asked.

"But that is different," she said. "I know how."

"Then you come out *with* me!" said Kevin, trying to sound spontaneous. He had to draw her away from the man, though there was still that other one, inside the cavern. If only he could get her on the bridge beyond both of them.

"No!" she protested, moving out onto the porch. "I must talk to you. I must know who you are and how you came here."

"I'll tell you," said Kevin, "but first, come out on the bridge with me. I've never been on one of these before." He turned and walked a few steps further out onto the bridge.

Whether the man behind her gave her orders to catch him, or whether she herself decided to gamble, he couldn't know, but suddenly she was running across the porch and down the stairs.

Remembering the man in the cavern, Kevin held his breath, but she came safely past it and onto the bridge. He glanced toward the headland. The fog was lifting, but his view was blocked by the tops of the trees.

"Hurry!" he whispered.

She walked toward him swiftly, holding onto the railings, and he saw mingled hope and anxiety in her face. Her eyes, he noticed, were green.

"Wait!" she called out, and her look told him this was for the benefit of the man behind the curtains.

Kevin turned and headed for the rock, moving as quickly as he dared on the precarious little bridge.

"Hang on tightly to the ropes," she whispered, behind him.

"Stop right there or I'll shoot!" a man's voice commanded.

"He was in the house," the woman whispered.

Without turning his head, Kevin asked "Shall we make a run for it?"

There was an ugly menace in the man's voice, but still they hadn't paused.

"Another step and I'll fire!" he shouted from closer range.

"I think he means it!" she whispered.

They stopped and looked back. He was standing at the landing of the bridge, pointing a gun at them. His eyes had the cold, calculating look of a killer.

"Now turn around and walk back here," he ordered, "and make it fast!"

Kevin's heart was pounding in his throat till he could scarcely breathe. His timing had failed. He'd moved too soon. If they walked back now, it was obvious they'd be surrendering themselves to a killer. He hesitated, still wondering if they should run for it and force the man's hand.

At that instant, the mysterious character in the cavern slipped out silently behind the gunman and conked him on the head with his club. The robber sagged to the ground without a sound, and his attacker took the gun from his limp hand.

"I knew I'd have need of a shillelagh!" he whispered, flinging down his driftwood weapon.

"Mr. O'Flaherty!" Kevin gasped in astonishment. "So it was you!"

"So it was!" said Terence O'Flaherty softly. "And you'd better be getting back in here behind me, both of you, till we see what's going to happen up there." He gestured toward the house with the gun he was keeping ready.

They hurried back to the landing, and the old Irishman reached out a helping hand to the lady and drew her inside, while Kevin slipped in behind her.

"How did you get here?" asked Kevin, still hardly believing his eyes.

"You're looking right at me, and you can ask?" said O'Flaherty. "Well, let me tell you, my lad, I'm not in the habit of taking a morning swim, fully clothed."

Kevin stared at him in the semi-darkness of the cavern and saw that his clothes were soaking wet. "You mean, you swam around the headland?"

"How else?" said O'Flaherty. "I didn't know what it was you had in your head, but it sounded pretty wild, and I didn't intend to let you go it alone. Only it was a mighty hard time you gave an old man, trying to catch up with you!"

"Oh, boy!" said Kevin. "You caught up just when we needed you most!"

From the house came the sound of shouting and scuffling.

"Sounds as if somebody else caught up, too," said O'Flaherty.

A moment later two officers appeared on the porch and Mr. O'Flaherty stepped out to meet them. "We've nailed this one," he said, "if you've got that one."

"We've got him," said one of the officers, kneeling down to put handcuffs on the unconscious bandit.

"All without a shot, and the lady safe," said O'Flaherty, "and we've got Kevin MacAlistaire to thank for it!"

"You mean—you knew?" the lady asked Kevin. "But how?"

"I was here last night, with my sister—"

"The rocks sliding!" she exclaimed, with sudden realization.

"And you played the organ," said Kevin.

"You knew, and stayed to help me?" she said.

"Swam out with his sister to call the police and came back, telling nobody what he was up to," said O'Flaherty.

The lady's eyes filled with tears, and she took Kevin's hands in hers, wanting to put her arms around him, but holding back.

"You are a brave young man!" she said, her voice breaking.

"That he is!" O'Flaherty agreed. "A bit daft," he added with a wink, "but brave all the same."

"And you, too, sir," she said.

"Terence O'Flaherty's the name, Ma-am—just an

170

old Irishman who'd risk his life any day of the year
for a beautiful green-eyed lady!"

The long ordeal was over, but there were still
some surprises ahead for Kevin and Christie. The
first came when their parents arrived at the old
mansion just after the police had taken away their
prisoners. With them they brought the man who
had been guest soloist at the benefit concert—
Michal Zagrodzky, the noted European pianist, who
had been touring the country.

Mr. Zagrodzky was as horrified as the Mac-
Alistaires to learn all that had happened in the
haunted cove, for the green-eyed lady was his wife.
She had been waiting in the old house to celebrate,
with him, their twentieth wedding anniversary.

In honor of the occasion, Terence O'Flaherty arranged a special dinner to be prepared by Mora's
mother. Mora helped serve it to all of them in the
huge dining room of the mansion. She confessed to
Christie that she was sure her spell had caused the
trouble, and she was through with witchcraft forever.

After dinner they all relaxed together in the enor-
mous living room with its two-story ceiling, and
Kevin noticed that the old organ was up on a bal-
cony overlooking the room, with gabled windows on
each side of it and a fireplace at one end. Plenty of
chance for drafts there, he thought, to account for
the ghostly sound.

As the hour of sunset neared, Christie asked Mrs.
Zagrodzky if she and Kevin and Mora could go out

with her to her rock. When she brought out her flute, they learned why her music was so special. Theodora Zagrodzky, their father told them, was one of the greatest flutists in the world. Though she was no witch, she played her instrument with a magic no one could match.

She put on her black cape with its sun and moon embroidered in gold, but one thing was missing—the most mysterious item of all: the green eye. Christie got up the courage to ask her about it, and she went to get it out of her jewel case.

The stone was a green oval set in gold, and it had the globe-like shape of a human eye. It was centuries old and very precious, and in the beginning it had been worn by a queen and blessed by holy men. Michal had given it to his wife as a wedding gift, and it was said to bring protection to its owner. Whether or not the jewel had anything to do with it, they all had to agree that on this day, Theodora Zagrodzky had been remarkably protected.

There was a gold chain that fitted around her head, and when she put on the green stone, it did indeed look like a third eye in the center of her forehead.

She took her flute and led them to the suspension bridge. "When I first saw that great rock rising out of the sea, I wanted so much to be out on it that I had to have the bridge built," she said. "But it is small. We will go one behind the other. I will lead the way, Christie, and then Kevin and Mora and Michal."

To their surprise, Michal Zagrodzky had appeared with a bucketful of fresh fish.

"I have it delivered to me every day," his wife explained. "The gulls and sea lions all expect their evening treat."

In single file, spaced well apart, they started across the little bridge. It swayed, and the walk seemed dizzying and perilous to Christie, but it was also very exciting. And when they reached the rock, it was like being on a ship at sea.

The clouds were beginning to glow with color when Mrs. Zagrodzky sent out three high notes on her flute.

"The sea lions are curious, and they like people," she said. "They have learned to come when I call with my flute. And the gulls—they stay always, for I feed them very often."

The gulls came down, a little shy of strangers, and stood waiting for their portion, and the sea lions came barging in to make a great splashing and foaming as they swam around the rock. Then Mrs. Zagrodzky blew the notes again, higher and thinner —first three and then seven—and far out they saw the dolphins arching in over the water.

Michal Zagrodzky fed the gulls and tossed the fish down to the creatures below, and when the feeding was over, his wife began to play the silvery melody Christie had heard before. The sea lions and dolphins leaped and whirled and vaulted as if they really were enchanted by her music, and before anyone realized it, the sun had set and it was growing dark.

Mora had a question. "Why do you always come out at sunset?" she asked Mrs. Zagrodzky.

"Because it is the time when day and night meet,"

she said, "and it gives me a special feeling of peace and beauty."

Christie could understand that, for she had felt it herself, but Kevin had another question.

"Have you ever seen any ghosts here?" he asked.

"Oh, yes, I often see the first Theodora sitting at the organ."

"Aren't you frightened?" asked Christie.

"No," said the green-eyed lady gently. "Why should I be? She's my great grandmother, and it's her organ."

ELIZABETH BALDWIN HAZELTON has had many years years of experience in writing for radio and television. Among other outstanding scripts, she has done a score of television screenplays for the series *Death Valley Days*. Miss Hazelton has also been a professional actress and for twelve years taught radio and television writing in Los Angeles. She now lives and works in South Laguna, California, in a house overlooking the Pacific Ocean. Her other books for young people are *Tides of Danger* (1967), *The Day the Fish Went Wild* (1969), *Sammy, the Crow Who Remembered* (1969), and *The Jade Eagle* (1970).